Bolan bulled his

Seconds later the hot air hit [illegible]
on the sidewalk. Behind him he heard the clatter of the doors, and several men burst outside, yelling in Chinese.

Bolan had sprinted halfway down the block when an alley appeared on his left. He veered into the darkness just as some bricks exploded next to his face. Then he heard the crack of the shots.

He found himself surrounded by tons of garbage in the dark. The Executioner thought this was as good a place as any for escape and evasion—until he reached a slight curve and realized the alley was a dead end.

Welcome to Hong Kong.

MACK BOLAN ®
The Executioner

#344 Primal Law
#345 Orange Alert
#346 Vigilante Run
#347 Dragon's Den
#348 Carnage Code
#349 Firestorm
#350 Volatile Agent
#351 Hell Night
#352 Killing Trade
#353 Black Death Reprise
#354 Ambush Force
#355 Outback Assault
#356 Defense Breach
#357 Extreme Justice
#358 Blood Toll
#359 Desperate Passage
#360 Mission to Burma
#361 Final Resort
#362 Patriot Acts
#363 Face of Terror
#364 Hostile Odds
#365 Collision Course
#366 Pele's Fire
#367 Loose Cannon
#368 Crisis Nation
#369 Dangerous Tides
#370 Dark Alliance
#371 Fire Zone
#372 Lethal Compound
#373 Code of Honor
#374 System Corruption
#375 Salvador Strike
#376 Frontier Fury
#377 Desperate Cargo
#378 Death Run
#379 Deep Recon
#380 Silent Threat
#381 Killing Ground
#382 Threat Factor
#383 Raw Fury
#384 Cartel Clash
#385 Recovery Force
#386 Crucial Intercept
#387 Powder Burn
#388 Final Coup
#389 Deadly Command
#390 Toxic Terrain
#391 Enemy Agents
#392 Shadow Hunt
#393 Stand Down
#394 Trial by Fire
#395 Hazard Zone
#396 Fatal Combat
#397 Damage Radius
#398 Battle Cry
#399 Nuclear Storm
#400 Blind Justice
#401 Jungle Hunt
#402 Rebel Trade
#403 Line of Honor
#404 Final Judgment
#405 Lethal Diversion
#406 Survival Mission
#407 Throw Down
#408 Border Offensive
#409 Blood Vendetta
#410 Hostile Force
#411 Cold Fusion
#412 Night's Reckoning
#413 Double Cross
#414 Prison Code
#415 Ivory Wave
#416 Extraction
#417 Rogue Assault
#418 Viral Siege
#419 Sleeping Dragons

Don Pendleton's

The Executioner®

SLEEPING DRAGONS

TORONTO • NEW YORK • LONDON
AMSTERDAM • PARIS • SYDNEY • HAMBURG
STOCKHOLM • ATHENS • TOKYO • MILAN
MADRID • WARSAW • BUDAPEST • AUCKLAND

First edition October 2013

ISBN-13: 978-0-373-64419-3

Special thanks and acknowledgment to
Michael A. Black for his contribution to this work.

SLEEPING DRAGONS

Printed in U.S.A.

I have learned to hate all traitors, and there is no disease that I spit on more than treachery.

—Aeschylus, circa 525–456 B.C.

A traitor betrays his country for many reasons, none of which is justified in my view. But when money changes hands and the traitor kills without remorse, the guy deserves a bullet to the brain.

—Mack Bolan

THE

MACK BOLAN

LEGEND

Nothing less than a war could have fashioned the destiny of the man called Mack Bolan. Bolan earned the Executioner title in the jungle hell of Vietnam.

But this soldier also wore another name—Sergeant Mercy. He was so tagged because of the compassion he showed to wounded comrades-in-arms and Vietnamese civilians.

Mack Bolan's second tour of duty ended prematurely when he was given emergency leave to return home and bury his family, victims of the Mob. Then he declared a one-man war against the Mafia.

He confronted the Families head-on from coast to coast, and soon a hope of victory began to appear. But Bolan had broken society's every rule. That same society started gunning for this elusive warrior—to no avail.

So Bolan was offered amnesty to work within the system against terrorism. This time, as an employee of Uncle Sam, Bolan became Colonel John Phoenix. With a command center at Stony Man Farm in Virginia, he and his new allies—Able Team and Phoenix Force—waged relentless war on a new adversary: the KGB.

But when his one true love, April Rose, died at the hands of the Soviet terror machine, Bolan severed all ties with Establishment authority.

Now, after a lengthy lone-wolf struggle and much soul-searching, the Executioner has agreed to enter an "arm's-length" alliance with his government once more, reserving the right to pursue personal missions in his Everlasting War.

Prologue

Chong Dia Marina, Hong Kong Island

Paul Rossi squatted in the semidarkness of the pier next to a large pillar and stared through his night-vision binoculars. Across the marina the speedboat churned up a small wake as it approached Eddie Lee's private yacht, the *Painted Lady*. Rossi felt the sweat running down his back but dared not move. The lookout, who was perched atop the small Plexiglas capsule over the yacht's cabin, appeared extremely vigilant. Rossi knew that any movement might attract the man's attention. Finally the lookout turned as the speedboat came alongside the yacht, and Rossi allowed himself a moment to relax and shift his position.

He checked his watch: 3:05. A hell of a way to spend a late night. Or an early morning, depending on your perspective. For him, it was the tail end of a very long day. He'd been shadowing Lee since midafternoon, when his sources had told him that the Triad arms dealer would be meeting with a "very special client." That in itself was enough to pique his interest, and he'd sent a text to his supervisors at Langley, Virginia, that he was following up on a lead. Then the real work had begun: doing a one-man shadow in one of the busiest cities in the world. Luckily, the magnetized tracking device on the inner fender of Lee's black Rolls-Royce limousine and a couple hundred Hong Kong dollars had led Rossi to Chong Dia Marina, Hong Kong Island.

The long trip by ferry from the main island had exhausted him, but he couldn't afford to be tired now. He would also have preferred to have a team on this surveillance, but with the Company's recent cutbacks and most of the Far East agents being either on the Mainland or keeping tabs on North Korea's latest nuclear plans, he had been forced to follow up on this recent lead himself. He smiled as he thought about being the Company's only man in Hong Kong. That was the way it felt sometimes.

The speedboat's motor whined to a halt as the smaller vessel drifted next to the yacht's aft. Rossi brought up the binoculars again. Four men on the speedboat… But the lights of the dock were too far away. They were only moving shadows even with the enhancement of the night vision. One of them was good-sized, the other two smaller in stature. There was something vaguely familiar about one of them, but what?

He had to get closer. The sentry on top was scanning the docks again. Rossi waited and, as the man's body turned away, did a quick trot to the next large pillar about thirty feet away. He flattened his back against it, holding the binoculars down in front of him, and began his waiting game once more.

He repeated this process three more times, each bringing him closer to the *Painted Lady*. The tapering sweep of the yacht's sleek hull was only about twenty yards away now and he was close enough to employ the BE-2700—the Bionic Ear listening device. He sneaked another quick check of the sentry and saw the man glancing in various directions. Rossi felt an incipient panic. Had the sentry seen him? Then, seconds later he felt a flood of relief as the night-vision binoculars showed the sentry remove a flat flask from his back pocket, unscrew the cap and take a few surreptitious sips. It had to be booze. Why else would he be so sneaky? Vodka, probably, to minimize the smell. Eddie Lee would most certainly lop off the man's head if he caught him drinking on the job. Or have his main bodyguard, Wang Sze, do it.

Rossi shivered at the thought. He'd seen Wang Sze from a short distance and the man looked very formidable—almost as wide as he was tall, with arms that burst out of the short-sleeved shirts he was fond of wearing.

Rossi checked the sentry again. The guy's posture looked more relaxed now than vigilant. Swallowing hard, Rossi decided on a bold move and did a crouching run to the boat next to the *Painted Lady*. It looked dark and unoccupied. But at three in the morning its owners could be sleeping if they were on board. Still, he couldn't hear as much if he stayed on the dock. He had to chance it.

Rossi checked the sentry again. The man's silhouette still showed him doing the relaxed lean against the back of the Plexiglas capsule's wall. He brought the flask up for another hit.

Good, thought Rossi, keep the imbibing going while I try to listen in on your boss.

He crept over the gangplank on tiptoe, the soles of his soft running shoes hardly making any noise. Keeping the cabin between him and the vessel, Rossi worked his way around to the prow and took up the best vantage point he could find. Cautiously, he set the duffel bag on the deck and pulled open the zipper. He took the BE-2700 out, slipped on the earphones and twisted the switch to the on position.

Static greeted his ears, so he tried holding the directional antenna at various positions until he finally heard the voices. To his surprise he heard words of English instead of Lee's Mandarin Chinese.

This makes things even easier, he thought.

But their words were still indistinct. Deciding to take the chance, Rossi crept forward in a modified crouch, keeping in the shadows as much as he could. He checked the sentry again. No change. Was he dozing?

I hope he's having a pleasant dream, Rossi thought as he pointed the antenna toward the *Painted Lady*'s cabin. This time the voices were clearer.

"I told you, the first shipments should be arriving shortly. The rest will be available soon. A few days at most. You must have patience."

It was Eddie Lee. Rossi recognized his Chinese-accented English.

"And as I told you," a second voice said, "I will make the next payment as soon as I have the shipment. My plan calls for a strict timetable. I cannot afford to wait."

This voice was definitely not Asian. More Middle Eastern. Arab maybe?

"Your timetable will be met," Lee said.

"And where are the technicians to train my men?" the Arab voice said. "The drones are useless to me without the ability to fly them."

"I assure you," Eddie Lee said, "they will be provided in due time."

Drones? Rossi suddenly realized he was onto something very big. But what?

"Time is a luxury I do not have," the Arab said. "I need results. I need the weapons."

A heavy wave slopped against the boats with a plop, obscuring the conversation and causing a slight rise and fall of the vessels. A passing freighter, no doubt, Rossi thought as he shifted his weight, still crouching, and strained his ears to hear more words.

"Do you think it is easy to obtain what you want?" Lee asked. "Do you know the risk I'm taking?"

"You are risking nothing compared to us," the other man said. "Our country has been overrun. Our very existence is in jeopardy. We must take it back."

Silence, then Lee said, "The Sleeping Dragons will assure your victory."

Sleeping dragons? Rossi wondered what they were talking about.

Suddenly another wave hit, larger than the previous one, causing both boats to rise higher. Rossi lost his balance momentarily, shifting his feet in a stutter step. He saw the sentry's head swivel and all at once the circular beam of a spotlight flashed outward from the capsule.

Rossi quickly danced backward, flattening against the exterior raised wall of his yacht's cabin. The illuminating beam cut through the night above him.

"What's going on?" he heard someone say in Chinese.

"I heard something over there," the sentry replied.

Rossi stuffed the BE-2700 back into his duffel bag. The light passed overhead again.

"Wang Sze," he heard Eddie Lee's voice say. "Check it out."

That didn't sound good, Rossi thought. Only one choice now.

As he ran toward the gangplank, he dumped the bag and its contents over the side and heard it plop into the dark water below. He thought about diving in himself but knew his chances for survival were better if he stayed on dry land. With the bit of a head start he had a slim chance. If he could get to the buildings that surrounded the marina, he could find someplace to hide. Rossi jumped onto the dock and sprinted toward the buildings a few hundred feet away, their lights like beacons beckoning him to shore. The night-vision binoculars bounced against his chest with every stride.

Behind him he heard voices and the clumping sounds of feet rapidly striking the wooden planks. They were on the dock now, chasing him.

Rossi came to the cyclone fence entrance, its gate still ajar from when he'd come inside. Glancing over his shoulder as he turned, he saw a group of four or five men, one of them powerful-looking, running full-out toward him. The burly one had to be Wang Sze. Rossi slammed the gate shut and flipped down the securing hatch. That would buy him precious seconds. He wished he had something to jam into the mechanism, then remembered the binoculars. He ripped the strap from around his neck and looped it through the opening between the two metal posts. He managed to repeat this one more time, figuring that was as many as he dared, and then jammed the binoculars down on top of the latch, working them between the metal posts and finishing with as hard a downward push as he could muster.

It should hold them for a bit, he thought.

They were only about fifty feet away now, and Rossi could see the large, flat face of the man he assumed to be Wang Sze leading the pack with an ominous grin stretching across his mouth.

Rossi turned and sprinted for the first set of buildings along the wharf—a small set of one-story structures where you could rent personal watercraft and buy other equipment. Farther down were a restaurant, gas station and more buildings, all closed at this hour. He glanced back over his shoulder. The group had stopped at the jammed gate and one of them had a knife out, sawing at the leather strap. Rossi heard a twanging sound and saw one man, Wang Sze, scaling the twelve-foot-high fence with the nimbleness of a gorilla. He twisted over the top and jumped down, landing lightly on the other side. From there he paused to rip the binoculars out of the juncture. He made it look effortless. Then he turned and began scanning the area.

Rossi just managed to swing around the corner of the nearest building. His breath was coming in ragged bursts and he paused for a moment to take out his small .380 Walther PPK. Perhaps he could pick a few of them off… He hesitated and then decided to wait. Letting them know he was armed would bring return fire.

He wanted to get help, but there was no one to call. Maybe get a message in, he thought. He had to let them know.

Crouching in the shadows, he fumbled through his pocket until he managed to get his satellite phone out and flip it open.

He couldn't risk calling in. They would hear his voice. He quickly pressed the buttons to the outbox section and sent a text: Eddie Lee—Sleeping Dragons.

Voices speaking Chinese. Close.

He flipped the phone closed and made another decision. If they caught him with the phone, they'd know he was with the Company and would trace back his calls. That would mean total disaster. Plus, if he could use the phone as a diversion… Cocking his arm, he reared back and pitched the phone into the darkness with all of his strength. From center field to home plate, he thought. He was rewarded with the sound of a thump and splash a few seconds later.

"You hear that?" one of his pursuers yelled. "He's by the water."

The group split up and Rossi took this as his chance to move. He turned and began running again, the silhouette of the next group of buildings perhaps thirty yards in front of him. His legs worked like pistons, pumping as hard as they could. The building loomed in front of him, twenty yards away… Fifteen… Ten…

He heard some heavy breaths behind him. Close behind him. Did he dare look back? He managed a fleeting glance. Wang Sze was perhaps five yards away and gaining, like an approaching locomotive. Rossi felt a chill run up his spine. He twisted his upper body, holding the Walther in his right hand and pointing it back underneath his pumping left arm. Pulling the trigger once, twice, he felt the weapon jump in his hand with each recoil. Wang Sze veered to the right, apparently avoiding the shots.

Maybe if I can turn, Rossi thought, I can hit him.

He slowed momentarily, whirling back toward his right,

pausing to dig his feet into the soft grass to allow himself the momentary stability to regroup, aim and fire. Bringing his right arm around in an arc, he raised the Walther and attempted to fix a sight-picture on the advancing Asian. But all he saw was darkness, then, in a peripheral flash he saw Wang Sze flying at him, his right leg fully extended, his left leg cocked underneath at an angle, his powerful arms jutting out like a boxer.

Rossi tried to adjust his aim as he fired but seconds later knew he was too late. The flying kick sent him tumbling backward, and he desperately sought to hold on to his gun. His back hit the ground first, knocking the wind out of him and sending him rolling in a somersault. As he rolled over onto his knees in a sitting position, he felt a wave of dizziness and accompanying nausea. Wang Sze was in front of him and Rossi brought his arm up again.

Did he still have the gun? He did.

His fingers curled around the metallic hardness, giving him momentary relief and hope. He blinked, trying to clear his vision so he could shoot the son of a bitch, but he saw the massive chest in front of him, only a few feet away. An arm lashed out and Rossi felt a hand as hard as steel smack against his own, sending the Walther flying from his grasp. He doubled up his left fist and sent a punch toward the other man's groin. Wang Sze shifted and Rossi's hand collided with a rock-hard slab of oblique muscle. He cocked back his right, ready to throw another haymaker, when the big Asian's body shifted again, and Rossi felt the ridge of the iron hand slam against the back of his neck.

A bright white star flashed somewhere inside his eyes, followed by an accompanying numbness as everything went black.

Northern Mexico

Mack Bolan, aka the Executioner, felt the increased sensory awareness he always felt just before the execution of a mission, but this time he felt something else, as well: a growing sense of wariness. The mission itself was difficult enough—rescuing a Mexican-American businessman's teenage daughter from a group of thugs who were holding her for ransom. But that wasn't what was causing his wariness. Bolan had been on so many missions that he was no stranger to risk and danger. What bothered him now was who accompanied him on this one: four young men from a private security agency known as the Bearcats.

The CIA and other covert agencies were relying on these private security firms more and more since the Iraq and Afghanistan wars, with varying results. Some of them were ex-G.I.s who had actual combat experience. Others, Bolan had learned, had been drummed out after the major reduction in forces and were sometimes lacking in "real time" experience under fire. He had his suspicions about this group and tagged them for the latter. Their leader, Kevin Norris, had bristled when told that Bolan would be in command of this mission.

"What?" he'd asked. "I thought I'd be heading things up."

No such luck, he'd been told, which had sent him into an extended sulk. Not a good sign, Bolan thought as he sized up the others: German Valdez, Tom Lipinski and Paco Dominguez. They kept calling him "sir," despite his protestations. All things considered, they'd performed reasonably well in the dry-run rehearsals the soldier had put them through in the hours leading up to the mission. But he wondered how they'd do when the balloon went up, how they'd react when they heard the sound of that first live round crackling by their ears. Bolan had been there and had seen it before. You never knew how someone would perform. Combat, like life, could be full of surprises, not all of them pleasant.

The Executioner probably wouldn't have signed on for this one had it not been for the girl. Maria Noval was only sixteen and had been abducted in front of her parents' plush home near San Diego. The kidnappers had brazenly driven her across the border and then contacted her parents with their ransom demand: one hundred thousand dollars. The accompanying threat of "No police, or else" put the parents on the edge of terror. Fearing for the life of their daughter, they'd paid. Then the next demand came: one hundred thousand more. The first one was only a down payment. To emphasize their point, the kidnappers had threatened to send one of the girl's fingers to them if they didn't pay within forty-eight hours.

That's when Mr. Noval had decided to call in a favor. As the owner of a large computer parts company, he had ties to the government. Since his company made the guidance components for the new Pegasus drones, eventually his problem reached the right people. But it was still a ticklish situation. Working across the border with the Mexican authorities, who were notoriously corrupt, was no assurance of a successful resolution. And in such a case, the U.S. government's hands were virtually tied. So someone had reached out even further and within twenty-four hours Hal Brognola had pinpointed the gang's location and briefed Mack Bolan and Jack Grimaldi on the operation.

"Four Bearcats are going on the mission," Brognola had

said. "The parents are insisting on it. Two are fluent in Spanish."

"What about the other two?" Grimaldi had asked. "They just along for the ride?"

"They come highly recommended," Brognola'd said.

And so here they were, creeping up on a fairly well-guarded compound in a remote area about fifty clicks west of Monterrey. The terrain was typical Mexico—lots of scrubs and cactus, sandy dirt and dipping arroyos. Bolan was thankful that it was mid-October and the usual heat of the summer season had dissipated. It was closing in on 0200 and he was also hoping that the cooler temperatures would minimize any unanticipated interaction with the indigenous hazards of the area like snakes, scorpions and Gila monsters.

He held up his fist as a signal for the rest of the squad to halt and surveyed the area ahead. The lights of the compound glowed in the night perhaps a hundred yards ahead through the scattered bushes and shrubbery. It was just as the satellite photos had depicted: three wooden-framed buildings set in a large, cleared-out circular area and surrounded by a ten-foot cyclone fence topped with concertina wire. The soldier turned and motioned to his squad.

"We'll proceed through this arroyo until we get closer," he said. "Then go along the fence line until we get to the entry spot. Once we cut through the fence, Valdez will take out the closest tower with the LAW. Then he and I will get the girl while the rest of you set up as planned. We clear?"

The other men nodded. They were looking a bit nervous now. Bolan had noticed it when they were painting up. The smell of raw sweat and fear. That's when the wariness had started to gnaw at him. How would these kids react if and when things got rough? And from what he'd heard about this gang, Los Lobos Negros or "the Black Wolves," it probably wasn't going to be smooth. He was glad he had his old pal Grimaldi as his flying ace in the hole.

Bolan keyed his throat mike. "We'll be in position in about five," he said.

"Roger that," Grimaldi's voice replied in Bolan's earphone. "I'll be there."

Bolan didn't know just how Brognola had gotten them the rocket-pod-equipped UH-60 Black Hawk helicopter for this one, and he didn't care. Somebody at Fort Hood or someplace was probably sitting on pins and needles at the moment, hoping for the equipment's safe return. But again, Bolan didn't care. All that mattered was that at the precise moment Grimaldi would sweep in and even the odds.

The soldier had his usual Beretta 93-R secured in a tactical holster on his thigh, and an H&K MP-5 submachine gun slung over his torso. Valdez, who was to hit the hostage site with Bolan, was similarly armed, but also carried a LAW. The others had sidearms and M-4 rifles with extra magazines. Light armament going in to facilitate rapid movement. In and out, with the Black Hawk as air support—it was a pretty good plan, but Bolan knew that the road to hell was paved with good intentions and even better plans.

When they were within fifty feet of the high cyclone fence that surrounded the compound, Bolan gave the signal for them to begin their low-crawl. They moved slowly so as not to attract any attention. The solider didn't know how alert the sentries in the guard towers would be at this hour of the morning, but detection before they were in position would mean certain death. They would take out the tower closest to them as soon as they were through the fence, and Grimaldi would be responsible for the rest. Bolan halted them again and flipped down his night-vision goggles to check the tower. No guard in sight. Not yet, anyway. That meant they still had the element of surprise. He brushed them back off his eyes.

They edged along the fence line to their established entry point position. The guard tower, about twenty yards ahead, still looked vacant. Bolan motioned for Lipinski to begin cutting the fence. It was a tedious task and the kid had balked at doing actual cutting each time during rehearsals.

"The more you practice what you know," Bolan had told him, "the more you'll know what to practice."

Lipinski had sucked it up after that, not complaining about anything.

Bolan looked at Valdez. "You ready?"

Valdez nodded, slipped off the end caps on the LAW and snapped it open, arming it. The sight popped up. Bolan watched to make sure the man kept the safety on for now.

Lipinski was clipping the last wires when Bolan keyed his mike again.

"Light them up," he said.

"Let there be light," came Grimaldi's reply.

The distant sound of the chopper's blades began cutting through the night and became progressively louder. Bolan grabbed the edge of the fence and was ready to pull it back at the precise moment. He did a quick study of their faces, colored dark by the camo paint, but still looking grim and nervous. It was almost showtime.

He heard the sound of a puffing runner inside the compound. Bolan looked and saw a heavyset man in blue jeans and an open fatigue shirt running toward the tower. The guy looked portly and out of shape, the tails of the open shirt billowing around his fat belly. If this was the caliber of their opponents, it should be a cakewalk. But the guy was carrying an AK-47. Heavy firepower. And Bolan gave the guy a few more points for attentiveness. Obviously, the sound of a helicopter was not something common to the nights out here.

The fat man cupped his hands, looked up toward the tower and yelled. No response. The man slipped the sling of the weapon over his right shoulder and began ascending the ladder, muttering to himself in Spanish. Bolan knew enough of the language to understand that the man was yelling and swearing at somebody. Probably the guard who was supposed to be awake in the tower.

Don't worry, pal, Bolan thought. He'll be up momentarily.

The first rocket from the Black Hawk streaked through the black night like a banshee holding a bottle rocket. The tower across the compound exploded in a yellow flash.

Bolan said, "Go!" and ripped back the fence. One by one they went through the hole, Valdez going first, slapping the safety off and aiming the LAW. A second later the rushing thrust of the emerging rocket and the fiery back-blast lit up their position. The tower exploded thirty feet above them, raining down clumps of broken wood and burned straw along with a man's body, which slammed down about sixteen feet away. The fat guy who'd been climbing the ladder had been knocked to the ground, too, landing on his back, the ladder on top of him, at a distance of maybe twenty feet from them. But the guy was tougher than he looked. He pushed the ladder away and unslung his rifle, his face twisting into an angry scowl as he sat up and brought the AK-47 to his shoulder.

Bolan was through the fence now and snapping the selection lever of his MP-5 to full-auto. The rest of his group stood frozen, waiting for directions, like four deer caught in the damn headlights.

"Move!" Bolan yelled, giving the closest one's shoulder a slap. He extended the MP-5 and sent a quick burst into the fat guy's chest. Nice weapon for a raid like this. Light, good ammo capacity, low recoil. The fat guy slumped backward into the dirt. Bolan shot a 3-round burst into the man's head for insurance and grabbed Valdez by the arm.

"Let's go. Get into your positions," he said, his voice a low growl, and began moving with Valdez toward the building where they believed the gang was holding the girl. The rest of the team members had snapped out of their temporary paralysis and were assuming their assigned cover positions. Bolan hoped that they wouldn't freeze again. At least not until the mission was over.

Hesitation was fatal in a moving op. Bolan had tried to drill that into the four men on the dry-run rehearsals he'd put them through. Norris had had a smirk each time he'd done the run-through. Bolan wondered if he was smiling now.

Two more rockets streaked overhead, and the soldier knew Grimaldi had taken out the other towers. Now he'd pull back and remain out of sight until they needed him for the final dust-off. Bolan flipped down his night-vision goggles. The scene turned to green images against a black background. Two more shirtless men began running from a nearby barracks. Bolan crouched as he flipped the lever back one to semi-auto and raised the MP-5 again. He put three rounds into each of them. He and Valdez ran toward the building. Over his shoulder he heard the distinctive popping sound of the M-4s. That meant Lipinski, Norris and Dominguez were in their respective positions and laying down cover fire. Twenty yards to go to the target building. Bolan glanced at Valdez, who was holding his MP-5 with both hands as he ran. His night-vision goggles were also in place.

Bolan released his machine gun, letting the sling suspend it in front of him. He reached to his pistol belt and took out a flash-bang grenade. They took positions on each side of the door, Bolan on the right and Valdez on the left. It was more of a flimsy wooden shack than a building, but the latch and padlocked hasp looked securely fastened to a solid door. It also made it the most likely place to keep a hostage. Bolan pulled the pin from the grenade as Valdez kicked the door hard. It caved inward, but surprisingly the hasp held in place.

Valdez swore and delivered another kick to the door. Once again, it jerked backward, but stayed secured. The man was looking winded. He stepped back, ready to deliver another kick, but this time Bolan joined him, swinging his right leg upward in an arcing motion so that the full sole of his boot smashed against the door with incredible force. This time the door flew inward, hit the wall and bounced back toward them again. Just as the door was closing, the soldier tossed the flash-bang through the narrow aperture. He turned his head as the brilliant flash lit the area and an explosion echoed inside the building.

The soldier went in low, curling to the left, followed by Valdez to his right. The fresh smell of burned cordite lingered in the air. Two figures were upright in a bed in the corner and one man stumbled around, holding a pistol. Bolan zipped a short burst across the stumbling man's chest. A girl's voice cried out. They were in the right place. Bolan turned and saw her, recognizing her face from the photograph. He also saw that her left leg was chained to the bedpost. The second figure, another shirtless man, was shaking his head and brandishing a long-barreled revolver. Bolan shot him once in the head and the man fell to the side of the bed.

"Carlos!" the girl yelled.

"We're here to help you, Maria," Bolan said. "Your father sent us."

The girl looked at him and screamed again. "Carlos! What have you done to Carlos?"

Oh, great, Bolan thought. The Stockholm syndrome. She'd been held for almost two weeks and longtime captives often developed a psychological bond with their captors, even if they kept them chained up like animals. Could anything else go wrong on this mission? he wondered.

Bolan glanced around the room, taking in the table, small refrigerator, few chairs and the second door on the other side. No more immediate threats. Outside he could hear the distinctive crack of AK-47 rounds.

"Sitrep," Bolan said into his throat mike as he gestured for Valdez to unchain the girl.

"Taking fire," Lipinski said. "Three hostiles down."

"I got two down," Norris added.

The firing ceased.

"*Uno mas* for me," Dominguez said. "No further movement at this time."

Assuming there was a man in each tower, that made a total of nine bad guys down. The satellite surveillance had recorded at least fifteen.

"That leaves six more unaccounted for," Bolan said, keying his mike. "Keep your eyes open."

Valdez was striking the thick wooden bedpost with the plastic stock of his MP-5, but it was having little effect. The girl screamed again.

"Hold her," Bolan said and stepped forward. He held the barrel of his MP-5 against the bedpost and emptied the remainder of his magazine in a sawing motion. The wood splintered as the stream of 9 mm projectiles disintegrated parts of it. When the magazine was empty, Bolan hit the release button, removed it and inserted a fresh magazine. He then brought his leg up to his chest and thrust the sole of his boot against the weakened bedpost. It broke with a splintering crack.

"Grab her," Bolan said, pointing to the girl. "Get ready to carry her. She may try to run from us. And put your weapon on safe."

Valdez nodded, doubling the length of chain around his left hand and holding out his arm.

"Let's go," he said to her.

"No." The girl struggled against him and Valdez recoiled in surprise. Bolan moved over and pinned her down, twisting her arms behind her back.

"Tie her hands," he said. "You'll have to carry her."

Valdez pulled a nylon strap from his pants pocket and began wrapping it around the girl's wrists. Bolan heard a stuttering of gunfire outside and keyed his mike again.

"Sitrep," he said, keying his mike.

"Taking fire position three," he heard Dominguez say.

Bolan went to the other door. It was open, and he glanced outside. Red and green tracers were streaking back and forth in front of the third building. This was bad. Position three was the last structure between them and the LZ at the far edge of the compound. Still, he had an ace to play.

"Jack," Bolan said. "We're ready to get out of here. Can you give us some help on quadrant three?"

"Been waiting for you to ask," Grimaldi said.

Bolan motioned for Valdez to bring the girl to the door.

"Bearcats, on my signal," the solider said into his mike, "pull back and rendezvous at LZ."

"Roger that," came the three replies.

Bolan listened to the syncopated chopping sound of the approaching Black Hawk. It turned into a high-pitched whine as Grimaldi banked in a sharp turn, hovering at an oblique angle above the third building. Opening up with the bird's twin miniguns, the stream of tracer rounds looked like a thousand fireflies descending. In seconds the walls were riddled with holes.

"You do good work, Ace," the Executioner said to his old friend.

"Like they say," Grimaldi answered, "I love it when a plan comes together."

The helicopter remained there a moment more, then zoomed toward the rear of the compound. Bolan watched as Valdez pulled the reluctant girl along. Finally, he bent over and stuck his shoulder against her waist, heaved her upward and began carrying her like a sack of jostling potatoes.

The soldier purposely slowed, making sure all of his team members were accounted for and heading to the rendezvous point. He saw Lipinski and Norris running up ahead. But where was Dominguez? Then he caught sight of him limping along.

Suddenly a figure rose from the darkness aiming a rifle.

Bolan brought his weapon up, too, squeezing off a quick burst. The gunner immediately fell.

Looks like there are still a few bad guys left after Jack's sweep, he thought as he got next to Dominguez.

"What's up?" Bolan asked.

"Hit in the leg," Dominguez said, his voice laced with pain.

Bolan looked down. Dominguez's right leg was oozing a steady flow. Each step was forcing more precious blood out, and they were still about a hundred yards from the LZ.

Bolan keyed his mike. "Norris, Lipinski, I'm bringing Paco back. Cover me."

With that he told Dominguez to halt. The kid was perhaps one-eighty so Bolan, figuring the easiest way was to imitate Valdez, stooped and cradled the other man over his left shoulder. That still left the soldier's right arm free in case he needed to use his weapon.

Bolan started a modified trot toward the LZ. Up ahead he could see Norris and Lipinski stationed on either side of the Black Hawk, its side door open with Valdez loading the girl inside.

Coming toward you, Bolan thought. Almost there. With a little luck and no more gunfire…

Thirty yards…twenty-five…twenty…

Lipinski's M-4 barked fire. Bolan could feel the rounds zip by him.

"Thought I saw movement over by quadrant two," he said.

Norris fired his gun, too. "I think so."

Bolan got to the door and leaned forward, placing Dominguez down on the smooth metal surface. "Get on board now," he said. Both Norris and Lipinski got up and scrambled into the bird. Bolan did one more quick survey through the night-vision goggles and said to Valdez, "Make sure she's secured."

He hopped through the opening and slammed the door shut, flipping the goggles back on his head. "Let's get the hell out of here." He leaned forward using his Ka-Bar to cut

Dominguez's pant leg. He checked the wound. It looked like a through-and-through.

"It's not too bad," Bolan told the kid. "You'll be all right." He tore open a combat bandage patch and slapped it over the holes.

Grimaldi glanced back over his shoulder and nodded, pulling back on the stick to start his liftoff. The chopper began to rise then momentarily hovered in place about sixty feet off the ground as three more rockets shot toward the array of wooden buildings. They erupted in fountains of red, orange and flaming yellow.

"I had a couple left over." His amplified voice echoed in Bolan's earphone.

The soldier grinned. He glanced over at the girl who stared back, her eyes open and vacant. Hopefully, she would be all right, too, once the shock of everything wore off.

"Hey," Grimaldi continued as the Black Hawk's sweeping ascent began to level out into a straight route for home. "I have a special treat for you guys." He leaned down and pressed the button on a big CD player that was wired into their radio frequency. Frank Sinatra's voice began singing "I Met Her in Monterrey" with Grimaldi doing an off-key accompaniment.

Bolan snorted and glanced at the girl again. He suppressed a chuckle and said, "It's a good thing you're such a hotshot pilot, Ace, because as a backup singer, you stink."

Stony Man Farm, Virginia

Mack Bolan hurried to the War Room at Stony Man Farm, his hair still wet from the shower. He and Jack Grimaldi had been in the middle of a workout in one of the outbuildings when word came down that something important had come up.

"Hal wants to see you in the War Room right away," Barbara Price had said. She'd given Bolan's sweaty form a once-over then flashed him a thumbs-up. "You're looking good."

"Thanks. Any idea what Hal wants?"

"Not a clue." She'd turned and started walking out of the gym. "Just that he needed to see you."

"Better you than me, pal," Grimaldi had said with a grin as he went back to punching the heavy bag.

"Actually, he wants both of you," Price returned over her shoulder. "ASAP."

Bolan had grinned back at Grimaldi. "Misery loves company."

About fifteen minutes later as Bolan walked into the War Room he saw Hal Brognola draping his suit jacket over the back of a chair. Staring at the end of an unlit cigar, his face wore a concerned scowl. Bolan knew better than to inquire if anything was wrong. He wouldn't have been summoned if something wasn't.

"Where's Jack?" Brognola asked without looking up. "I wanted him here, too."

"He's on his way. Even after all this time he still hasn't mastered the art of a three-minute shower."

Brognola grumbled, stuck the unlit cigar in his mouth and looked at his watch. He picked up a ceramic cup that had been sitting on the table and took a sip. After another scowl he shook his head.

Bolan smiled. Brognola's expression meant that Aaron "the Bear" Kurtzman was nearby. His near-toxic coffee was legendary at Stony Man Farm.

Grimaldi strolled into the War Room with a wide smile. "I miss anything?"

"Just the page I sent out for you thirty minutes ago," Brognola said, taking a seat.

"We were in the gym," Grimaldi replied, rotating his head. "Needed to work out a few kinks after our last mission."

Brognola chewed the cigar some more, took another sip from the mug, then motioned for them to sit. "The Company apparently lost an operative in Hong Kong."

"When?" Bolan asked.

"Last night," Brognola answered. "A guy named Paul Rossi. Cause of death is listed as accidental—a car accident."

"Is foul play suspected?" Grimaldi asked.

Brognola snorted. "Foul play? Can the euphemisms. Recently he'd been shadowing a Chinese national named Lee, Wan Hong, aka Eddie Lee, aka Eddie 'Boom-Boom' Lee."

"Boom-Boom?" Bolan said. "As in Chinese firecrackers?"

Brognola nodded. "The very expensive kind. Lee's connected to the Triads and has a pretty substantial reputation as an arms dealer."

"Anything specific on why Rossi was following him?" Bolan asked.

"Nothing solid. Just that Lee's been rumored to be having meetings with some new client," Brognola said. "Nobody knows who, but something seems to be going on."

"Something's always going on over there," Grimaldi said. "Why are we getting involved?"

"Somebody in Wonderland called in a marker. The CIA is stretched real thin over there. Most of their operatives are either in Bejing or trying to keep watch on North Korea's latest nuclear rumblings. Rumor has it their current Great Leader is threatening to flex his muscles a bit."

"Yeah, I heard something about that," Grimaldi said. "Say, is he Great Leader number two or number three?"

"He's number two, definitely," Bolan said. "What else do we know about this Rossi-Lee thing, Hal?"

Brognola picked up a manila folder that was on the table and opened it. He took out two glossy, eight-by-ten pictures and handed one to Bolan. "This is Eddie Lee."

Bolan studied the picture for a few seconds: Asian male, mid- to late-forties, thin, waspish features sandwiched between the high cheekbones. He handed it to Grimaldi.

"Proper name's Lee Wan Hong," Brognola said. "As I mentioned, he's also known as Eddie Lee and Boom-Boom Lee. He was born and raised in Hong Kong and has been with the Wang Shun Triad group since the mid-eighties when he ran numbers and did kickback collections for them. He was gradually upgraded to an enforcer and got his own gang. He has family ties on the Mainland and travels there frequently. He's also got an older uncle who was very high up in the military through the 1997 transition. The uncle apparently introduced Boom-Boom to the right people, and suddenly little Eddie graduated from making numbers collections to selling weapons."

"What kind of weapons?" Bolan asked.

"He started out small, peddling AK-47s and old Makarov and Tokarev pistols to the local hoodlums. Then he opened his own import-export business and expanded to neighboring countries selling anything and everything from Kalashnikovs to RPGs to radical elements in Indonesia, the Moro Islamics in the Philippines, and then some." Brognola smiled. "He's done quite well—a regular Chinese Horatio Alger."

"Go west, young man," Grimaldi said.

"East, west and every other direction he can, from the sound of it," Bolan added. "But the quote's from Horace Greeley, not Alger."

"Whatever," Grimaldi said. "The guy sounds pretty capitalistic for a Commie." He pointed to Brognola's coffee mug. "You make that?"

Brognola shook his head. "Aaron."

The Stony Man pilot frowned.

"Where else has Lee been peddling his wares?" Bolan asked.

"You name it," Brognola said. "We've had reports he's opening pipelines to other regions like Somalia and some other hot spots.

"And this," he added, handing Bolan a second photo, "is Wang Sze, Lee's number-one bodyguard."

Bolan studied this picture, also. Another Asian, but younger than Lee and with a more formidable look. The high, wide planes and large chin gave the face a brutish cast. The broad nose looked as though it had been broken more than once, and the sweep of the thick neck suggested it was attached to a powerful body.

"Looks like a mean son of a bitch, doesn't he?" Brognola said. "Well, take it from me, he is. He's a bodybuilder, boxer and martial artist."

"Besides being an expert thug, no doubt," Grimaldi said.

Brognola propped the cigar at the side of his mouth. "This guy's the real deal, all right. He was Mr. Hong Kong a few years back, and also the heavyweight boxing champ of Hong Kong as well as a master of kung fu. He was knocking out all comers on the underground fighting scene, and then was recruited by Eddie Lee to work exclusively for him."

Bolan studied the face a moment more then passed that photo to Grimaldi, as well.

The pilot emitted a low whistle. "Never win first prize at the Hong Kong beauty pageant."

"What about Rossi?" Bolan asked. "Was he reliable?"

Brognola nodded. "Supposed to have been a stand-up guy. Ex-Marine."

Bolan nodded. "That's good enough for me."

"Me, too," Grimaldi said, "except that there's no such thing as an ex-Marine."

Brognola smirked. "Yeah, I know."

"Any theories as to why they iced Rossi?" Bolan asked.

"As I said," the big Fed continued, "Rossi's death was officially listed as an accident. But Lee's got a reputation for being the go-to guy in the region for any type of small- to medium-size weapons. About a week ago Rossi notified his superiors at Langley about rumors that something more substantial was in the works. Something big. He was following Lee and ended up the victim of a hit-and-run on Hong Kong Island."

"I'll bet there's a lot of those over there," Grimaldi said. "After all, they drive on the wrong side of the road, don't they?"

"They were taught by the Brits," Bolan said. "Anything more substantial?"

Brognola shook his head.

"Shouldn't this be a CIA matter?" Bolan asked. "I mean, if Rossi was one of theirs."

Brognola took the cigar out of his mouth and sighed heavily. "Yeah, yeah, I know. But like I said, somebody in Wonderland pulled in a marker. The agents they do have in the region are already run ragged, and with all the important trade we got going with China right now, it's in the best interests of the country to have this matter looked at in, how can I say it?" He reinserted the cigar, looked at them and smiled. "An unofficial manner."

Bolan grinned. "You're even starting to sound like a Washington bureaucrat."

"Bottom line, we need somebody to go over there fast and find out what's going on. Interested?"

Bolan nodded. "Count me in."

Brognola looked at Grimaldi, who grinned. "Just one question. Can we take *Dragonslayer* with us?"

Brognola snorted. "I took the liberty of assuming you two would be on board. Aaron's fine-tuning all the logistics now. He's arranging a cover for you. Company executives looking to import a new line of toys."

"Toys?" Grimaldi queried.

"Lots of those in Hong Kong," Bolan said. "Especially the kind Eddie Lee deals in."

"So for the moment, you're going commercial," Brognola said. "Once you get on the ground you can tag up with an operative from MI-6 named Winston Cleeves. He has a lot of local connections. Supposed to have been their top man over there for some time."

"Makes sense," Bolan said. "The Brits have been a long-established foothold in Hong Kong."

"Even if they did teach them to drive on the wrong side of the road," Grimaldi added.

"Quit horsing around and get ready to shove off," Brognola said. "They're warming up the plane now."

"Hal," Bolan said, "do you have anything else for us?"

"As a matter of fact, I do," Brognola said, leafing through the folder. "Right before Rossi met with his most unfortunate *accident,* he sent a four-word text on his satellite phone back to Langley."

"Four words?"

Brognola nodded. "'Eddie Lee—Sleeping Dragons.'"

"Sleeping dragons?" Bolan asked. "What does that mean?"

Brognola sat back in his chair. "That's what I hope you two guys are going to find out."

IN THE COMFORT of his plush, back-room office inside the Wong Tu Do Mahjong Parlor and Restaurant, Eddie Lee used the mouse to move the black stone two spaces ahead on the board, capturing the white piece. The computer responded with an alternate move, capturing one of his blacks. He lamented the lack of quality human opposition to play real game matches of *weiqi* and mahjong, but his underlings were no challenge anymore. They all played like women, afraid not to let him win for fear of retribution. There was no challenge. At least playing on his computer afforded him some degree of intrepid competition.

He picked up the piece of plain white paper and made the first fold as he glanced through the large one-way glass window that provided him a covert view of the evening's activities in the main part of the parlor. Busy for a Wednesday night, he mused as he watched the hostesses pouring drinks and the men laying down piles of money and chips on various bets. Lee made the second and third folds of the paper. His thoughts ultimately turned to the main task at hand: obtaining the Sleeping Dragons. He was growing weary of dealing with the fanatical Arab. The man was a borderline psychopath, and Lee was not sure if, in the end, Mustapha Shahkhia could be trusted.

He smiled. Perhaps Shahkhia had inherited some of his purported biological father's emotional instability. Although he was officially listed as the son of the deceased Colonel Ahad Shahkhia, Mustapha privately claimed to be the illegitimate son of Libya's former "Great Leader." Muammar Khadaffi, the story went, had sent his former friend and fellow military commander away to allow him to seduce Shahkhia's pretty young wife. She, too, was dead, and eventually

Khadaffi had gone to meet them both somewhere on the plains of their desert eternity so the truth would never be known.

Lee didn't care one way or the other, as long as the man's money was good. Speaking of which, it was time to check on his finances. He terminated the game and clicked over to the internet to check his banking records. The money transfer from the Arab's Swiss accounts still had not gone through. The bastard was making good on his threat to hold things up until he had the shipment. And what would his reaction to this latest development be once Shahkhia found out the Americans were involved, given his pathological hatred of them? They had, after all, been ultimately responsible for the death of his father. Lee smiled. Actually, for both his fathers.

But one thing *weiqi* had taught him was to make sure all his options were properly addressed and fortified. Leave nothing to chance. Lee finished making the fifteen folds and the paper dragon took shape. He set it down next to the mouse and clicked to another screen ready to send an email to his uncle, then reconsidered.

Better not to leave any traceable trail, even electronically, he thought.

He used his cell phone instead, sending a text: Dear Uncle Yu I wish very much to see you. Short and to the point. Also in their established code addressing him as "Dear Uncle." The general would know that Lee's request was urgent. He slipped his cell phone closed, set it down on his desk and pressed a button on his intercom.

"Yes, boss," the voice said.

"Send in Wang Sze."

"Right away, boss."

Lee pressed his fingers together in a steeplelike gesture and leaned forward in concentration. So many different factors, all spinning in the air in front of him… He remembered seeing a circus juggler once on the Mainland as a child. The man kept five apples in constant rotation in front of him with what appeared effortless motion. As the crowd watched, the juggler suddenly grabbed one of the pieces of fruit, took a bite and sent it back into the air, never missing a beat. Lee smiled at the memory—such dexterity, such coordination. Now it was his turn to be the juggler, using people instead of apples. He wasn't sure how much the Americans knew, but he had to find out.

The door to the office opened, and Wang Sze stepped through. He was so broad-shouldered that he turned sideways to keep from brushing against the sides of the doorway. Wang Sze stopped in front of the desk and raised an eyebrow.

Lee lowered his hands and stared back at him. "We have a new problem. We must prepare for some special visitors."

Wang Sze kept the eyebrow elevated and canted his head slightly.

"The Americans are coming," Lee said, "to investigate the late Mr. Rossi's tragic accident."

Wang Sze smiled and nodded, then his face twisted into a snarl and he snapped his right fist against his open left palm. The snarl left his face and his head canted again as a sign of respect for his boss. It was punctuated by another questioning look.

Lee shook his head. "No, not yet. I have to find out what Rossi told them."

Wang Sze gave him another questioning look and cocked a thumb toward his huge chest.

"No, not you." Lee held up the folded paper dragon and said, "See that this is dropped off at the usual place." He waited a moment more, then added, "And get me Simmons."

Wang Sze nodded and bowed. "It will be taken care of, boss."

Jillian Danser held on to the plastic-coated handrail and felt herself sway with the motion of the bus. She wasn't the only female standing, but she was the only Caucasian. The majority of the seats were taken up by Chinese men who were either reading their newspapers or texting on their smartphones.

Not a gentleman in the lot, she thought, and wondered how she might fare if she were still back in London riding the bus.

Probably not much better, but it was pretty to think so.

It was almost as pretty as thinking about the dashed dreams she had, too. Dreams of travel, exotic locales, adventure and excitement. That was what she'd thought when she'd been accepted into government work and gotten assigned to MI-6. Being recruited in college for British intelligence had filled her head with notions of saving the world while racing against a ticking clock—the stuff celluloid dreams were made of, she now knew. After spending five long years in the home office doing little more than filing, report writing and a few boring surveillance details, her transfer to the Hong Kong office had finally come through.

She'd been so excited. It had seemed like the fulfillment of her dreams, until, that is, she arrived in the overly crowded, foul-smelling city. Hong Kong, or "fragrant harbor," as it was translated. It was fragrant, all right. Incense, rotting wood, noxious sewers and equally disgusting food. She was surprised they didn't use garlic and peppers in their tea.

And she was equally dismayed at the nature of her assignments. Certainly, she was the junior agent here, and a woman to boot, but her supervisor, the ever-efficient Winston Cleeves, made it clear from day one that she would be considered an "equal member of the team."

Good old Winston, she thought, giving her such a plumb of an assignment, especially when she knew he'd sent Fawkes to the New Territories to check on something involving Eddie Lee. She was, as he never failed to put it, "An important and indispensable member of Her Majesty's team here in Hong Kong."

The game's afoot, she thought, that's for sure.

But she never thought that this game would be even more boring than her London duty had been. It usually consisted of being Cleeves's number-one gofer, getting copies of reports and picking up lunch for "his majesty." Well, that was doing the queen a bit of disservice. Cleeves certainly wasn't royalty, but his status here as the preeminent British agent in Hong Kong gave him delusions of a similar magnitude.

The bus crept forward a few feet then stopped abruptly. Jillian felt herself get jerked in both directions.

Even the damn buses have it out for me, she thought. But I should try to look on the bright side. At least it's a nice evening.

The sun was beginning to set and the ubiquitous glow of neon lights was starting to wink on throughout the myriad shops beyond the bus windows.

In a few hours she'd have to be at the airport for her rendezvous. She wondered what he would be like. Cleeves had been customarily brief in his directive.

"The Yanks are coming," he'd said. "At least one of them is. Go to the airport tonight and collect him. Be there at 2100. His name is Matt Cooper."

She'd written the name down along with the flight arrival time and information. It was still several hours away, but she was curious as to what this new addition to her boring routine would be like.

Matt Cooper, she repeated mentally. Probably short, fat and leads a pitifully boring life just like I do.

BOLAN WOKE UP as the plane banked slightly and the pilot's voice came over the intercom first in Chinese and then English saying that they were beginning their descent into Hong Kong airport. Over the years he'd mastered the art of catching a combat nap when the situation presented itself, and being on a transpacific flight offered little else. The soldier raised the window shade and glanced down at the triangular landmass that jutted from the adjacent island mass. As the plane circled he could make out the distant skyline of the symmetrical peaks of a seemingly endless array of skyscrapers.

He stretched and mentally reviewed the events of the past seventeen hours—the flight from Arlington to San Francisco where he and Grimaldi had split up after checking in on his satellite phone with Stony Man Farm from an airport bar. The conversations replayed in his mind.

"Good news and bad news," Aaron "the Bear" Kurtzman had said. "Which do you want first?"

"Surprise me," Bolan said.

"You and Jack are going to have to split up. I've got him booked on a separate flight to Osaka." Kurtzman paused and Bolan could almost see him taking a sip of his horrible coffee. "However, he'll be picking up a private jet in Japan and flying it to Hong Kong so you guys will have some mobility getting out of there."

"What's the bad news?" Bolan asked.

He heard Kurtzman's snorting laugh. Grimaldi, who was sitting on the adjacent bar stool, shot him a quick look.

"The Limeys will send someone to meet you," Kurtzman said. "Not sure who, but the main guy's name is Winston Cleeves."

"How will I know them?"

Kurtzman snorted again. "How the hell should I know? You want me to fax you a picture or something?"

"Just don't fax mine," Bolan quipped.

"Yeah, right. They should be expecting you, Mr. Cooper."

"Sounds good," Bolan said. "I'll fill Jack in."

"Do that," Kurtzman stated. "In the meantime, I've already sent him an email with all the details."

"Fill me in on what?" Grimaldi asked as soon as Bolan had hung up.

"That Santa got your letter and is leaving you a little present in Japan, where you're going now."

Grimaldi looked expectant. "What kind of present?"

"A plane," Bolan said. He pointed to Grimaldi's vibrating smartphone.

Grimaldi picked up the device and read the message. He shook his head in disgust.

"What's the matter?" Bolan asked. "You always seem happiest when you're flying yourself."

"Yeah," Grimaldi said, holding up the smartphone, "but if I would've known he was setting me up, I'd have asked him to send me *Dragonslayer* instead."

"Well, we are supposed to be dealing in toys."

Grimaldi picked up his drink and drained it. "Guess I'd better get over to my new gate," he said. Then he stopped and pointed at the TV above the bar. "Hey, pal, turn that up, will you?"

A cable news station was showing a tape of an extremely beautiful woman dressed in an elegant tan pantsuit being interviewed by a reporter. The scrolling type along the bottom proclaimed INTERNATIONALLY KNOWN ACTRESS CELISE BOYER NAMED UNITED NATIONS GOODWILL AMBASSADOR—TO VISIT LIBYA TO CHECK ON HUMANITARIAN AID EFFORTS. The bartender grabbed the remote and hit the volume.

"I'm so looking forward to working with the NTC and seeing the further positive results of what happened during the Arab Spring," the woman said breathily. "And I'm looking forward to seeing how conditions have improved for the people."

Grimaldi made a clucking sound and winked. "Celise Boyer." He dragged out the last name—*boy-yay,* using the French pronunciation. "Man, is she a babe, or what?"

"I don't know," Bolan said. "She's got more tattoos than a Navy lifer."

Grimaldi snorted as he scrunched up his face. "Yeah, right. I've seen all her movies. What I wouldn't give to have a date with her."

"Just remember to keep your pants on when you get to your new gate," Bolan said.

Grimaldi's grin stayed in his mind as the plane banked again and Bolan felt the deceleration begin as he heard the grating sound of the landing gear being lowered. The touchdown that subsequently followed was a bit rough, bouncing twice before evening out.

I hope that wasn't a sign of things to come, Bolan thought.

"Ladies and gentlemen," the pilot's voice said in English, "welcome to Hong Kong."

MUSTAPHA SHAHKHIA SAT hunched on the bed in his hotel suite dipping his fingers into the greasy rice cake and bringing periodic bundles to his mouth. But now his appetite had ceased. The longer he watched the rebroadcast of the television news interview, the more incensed he became. The scrolling message under the woman's face identified her as internationally known actress Celise Boyer, some sort of United Nations Goodwill Ambassador. Her voice, as haughty and sinful as a strumpet's, shoveled more fuel on his growing rage. "I'm so looking forward to working with the NTC and seeing the further positive results of what happened during the Arab

Spring. And I'm looking forward to seeing how conditions have improved for the people."

The NTC—National Transitional Council, puppets of the West Arab spring… Shahkhia could take no more. It was the same Western news channel that had so callously shown the torture and murder of the Great Leader—his real father—at the hands of the militia forces. Had they no shame? No decency? No respect?

He reached for the nearest solid object, in this case the hotel phone, and hurled it toward the woman's telephonic image. The screen buckled and chipped upon impact, losing the picture but giving off an ominous hissing sound. His anger not yet sated, Shahkhia followed by throwing his teacup and then the still-full metal pot. This time the screen exploded, littering the rug with myriad glass slivers. This second noise brought the man's faithful bodyguard, Abdul Sultan, running into the bedroom from the outer room. The giant paused at the door and looked at the shattered TV.

"Is everything all right, Sheikh?" Sultan asked, his huge hands at the ready to withdraw his dagger or his gun.

"Celise Boyer," Shahkhia said. "I cannot wait until we rule the world with Sharia law and can have all such filthy whores stoned to death in the public square."

Sultan's face showed no emotion.

Shahkhia picked up the metal tray of food and hurled that against the wall. He looked back at his bodyguard. "Are you certain there was no pork in that meal?" His voice was a roar.

Sultan nodded and said, "Yes, sir. They assured me of such."

Shahkhia kicked the tray. "Get someone to clean up this mess." He glanced at his watch. "Soon it will be time for prayers." He shot his companion a spiteful look. "I grow weary of this land of the Chinese pagans. I feel like I'm making a deal with Satan's disciples."

Sultan smiled slightly. "Yes, sir, but better the devil you know..."

"The devil I know, all right." Shahkhia stepped over and gave the dented tray another swift kick. He wasn't a particularly big man, but he prided himself on being nimble. The tray crashed against the wall again and he felt a surge of satisfaction.

"Is there any word from Sirte? Have the drones arrived?"

Sultan shrugged. "I was checking for the emails when you...when I heard the noise."

Shahkhia's lip curled downward, and he raised his fists above his head as he spoke. "I swear by God and all that is holy that I will return to the land of my father and my father's father and drive the puppets of the infidels into the fires of hell."

Abdul Sultan stood patiently by the door. Shahkhia lowered his arms, stared at him and closed his eyes to slits. His head rocked slightly as he recited a prayer from the Koran, then held his palms out toward the other man. "My faithful Abdul, son of my father's strong, right arm, and now my sword, as well. Where would I be without you by my side?"

Sultan bowed slightly, touching his forefinger to his forehead, and then offered his palm in supplication. "By your leave, I shall do as you've ordered." He turned away.

"What? Where are you going?"

The bodyguard stopped, turned and said, "To the front desk. I must see to the cleaning."

Shahkhia then realized he'd destroyed not only the television but the telephone, as well, when he'd ripped it out of the wall. Instruments of Satan, both of them. He nodded and made a brushing gesture with the fingers of his right hand.

His rage began to subside. He listened as Sultan closed the door as he left. The tedious nature of these negotiations, and the duplicitous Eddie Lee seemed to be eating away at his reserves of equanimity. He smiled to himself. Not that he'd ever had much of that.

I am my father's true son, he thought, then began to think about his official father and the ignominious death he had suffered. Colonel Ahad Shahkhia, the man whose name he had taken and whose name was on his certificate of birth, had been killed by the Americans in 1985. That alone would have been justification for his jihad. But Shahkhia knew the truth, told to him by his mother shortly before her death.

"You are the son of the Great Leader," she said. "It is why we named you Mustapha."

The Great Leader was wise and knew that the son he had sired was a true warrior to be taken and groomed as his successor. The Great Leader knew the value of both blood and loyalty. He'd taken Mustapha at an early age and made sure he was treated well, and trained by the finest teachers and educated in the ways of the pen and the sword. Mustapha knew that the Great Leader viewed him not only with legitimacy but with favor, as well. Why else would he have trusted Mustapha to go with his "half brother" to Europe? Why else would he have been trusted with the information about the Swiss accounts? And now, with his half brother in the custody of the puppets, it was up to Mustapha to uphold the family honor and the way of God. It was up to him to take his country back.

But to do that he needed to follow his game plan. He needed to obtain both the new, specialized drones and the Sleeping Dragons. In short, he needed to continue his deal with the devil. He needed Eddie Lee.

4

Jillian Danser kept the cell phone pressed to her ear, trying to listen with as much circumspection as she could muster as Winston Cleeves gave her the final instructions regarding the arriving American. It wasn't an easy task, considering the damned muffler on the bus had to have had a hole in it the size of soft drink can, and the woman was certain the seat she'd scooped was right over it. Plus the blasted vehicle was still so crowded that there were no other seats available.

"Are you hearing me all right, my dear?" Cleeves asked. "Where on earth are you, by the way?"

"I'm on the bus, sir," she said.

"The E-Eleven?" There was a lengthy pause. Cleeves was prone to the dramatic. She heard him clear his throat before he continued. "Ah, well, your frugality shall be duly noted in your next review. But do try to step it up a bit when you get to the airport. You know how those Yanks hate to be left waiting."

"Yes, sir," she said. "I believe you were telling me how I'm going to recognize them."

"Was I? Yes, I believe I was, as well." Cleeves laughed. He always seemed to enjoy his own jokes. "First of all, as I mentioned previously, tonight you'll only be meeting one man. The other will be arriving sometime tomorrow. Are you following?"

"I am, sir."

"Ah, brilliant. Now this man you're meeting tonight, who should be arriving within the hour, is purportedly a big fellow with dark hair. Once again, his name is Matt Cooper. I suggest you have him paged or stand with some sort of sign." He paused again and took a sonorous breath. "I'll leave the details to you. At any rate, you're to accompany him to his hotel. I'm sure he'll be a bit worn down from traveling so we'll plan on getting into full swing tomorrow."

"Yes, sir," she said. "Anything else, sir?"

"Presumably." His voice was redolent with sarcasm. "Since I prefaced my phrase by saying, 'first of all.'"

Danser was used to Cleeves's little digs and waited. This, too, shall pass, she thought.

"Second," he said, stressing the word, "the designated password sequence to confirm his identity will be as follows…" A few seconds passed. "Danser, are you ready to receive?"

"I am, sir."

"Very well. Once you've made initial contact with Mr. Cooper, he will ask, 'Can you take me to Winthrop Harbor?' You will then reply with the phrase, 'By train, plane or automobile.' Are you following?"

"All the way, sir," she said.

"Good. Call me when you've successfully established contact."

Danser said she would and terminated the call, blowing out a long breath and pressing back against her seat.

Did the man think she was a complete idiot?

Winthrop Harbor. Did such a place actually exist? Probably, but not here in Hong Kong. This superfluous clandestine circumlocution had Cleeves written all over it. He was, after all, old school, and took particular delight in reminding every new charge who served under him that he was the longest-serving British agent in Hong Kong. She could attest to him not only being the longest serving, but the most boorish, as well.

Danser allowed herself a giggle at the thought of her supercilious supervisor being told that he was indeed a boor. Perhaps someday, at his retirement party, she'd make it clear what she thought of him.

It'll give me something to look forward to, she thought as she glanced at her wristwatch. Plenty of time remained before she had to meet the American version of 007 and help him save the world. She giggled again at the ludicrousness of that prospect.

BOLAN HAD CLEARED customs and was walking down the gleaming main aisle of the terminal. He continued toward the baggage claim area, but there was no need for him to stop there. A lifetime of being on the go and traveling light allowed him to fit everything he needed into his carry-on. Going through customs had been a breeze. Mr. Matthew Cooper, toy company executive, here on business, had nothing to declare, nothing except the clothing and toiletries in his carry-on. The rest of his equipment, no doubt, had been sent via diplomatic courier directly to the American Embassy. He'd have to stop there the next day. At the moment, he needed to touch base with Stony Man Farm. As he stepped onto the moving walkway, he took out his secure satellite phone and checked for messages. There was one from Aaron Kurtzman saying to check with Hal Brognola for the password. Bolan deleted it then called the big Fed's number.

It rang several times, passing through several cutouts, before Brognola answered with a grunt.

"Was that supposed to be a hello?" Bolan asked.

Brognola snorted. "Christ, you know what time it is?"

One walkway ended and Bolan stepped onto another, confirming, "2029."

"Yeah, well, it's 0729 here. And I didn't get to bed till five."

Bolan chuckled, imagining Brognola fumbling through the bedside table for a new cigar to chew on.

"Give me a break, will you? I've been in the air for the past twenty-some hours or so."

Brognola grunted again, and Bolan figured he'd either found the cigar or was starting to wake up. "Any updates on my meeting with MI-6? Aaron's message said something about a password."

"Yeah, yeah, I know." Brognola made a few more grumbling sounds then said, "Okay, here it is. They're looking for you under your current name. You're to ask them, 'Can you take me to Winthrop Harbor?' Your contact will reply, 'By plane, train or automobile.' Leave it to the Brits. Always into all that clandestine stuff."

"Where the hell's Winthrop Harbor?" Bolan saw the large blue sign spelling out in English and Chinese to take the escalator down to the baggage claim and main terminal area. He stepped onto it.

"Doesn't matter," Brognola said. "They're the ones who came up with it."

"Any idea who will be meeting me?"

"No, but I have the utmost confidence you'll be able to figure that out."

Bolan grinned. "Okay, I'll check back and give you a sitrep once I get settled."

"Oh, swell," Brognola said. "Wake me up again at dawn, why don't you?"

"I'll do my best," Bolan said and terminated the call. The escalator ended, as well, and he stepped off, scanning the moderately crowded airport. Bolan knew this airport, Chek Lap Kok, had opened in 1998 and had one of the largest passenger terminals in the world. Finding someone he didn't know would be problematic so he'd have to let the person find him. Chances that Kurtzman had sent MI-6 his picture were slim and none. The man had too much savvy for that.

Plus, the British were pretty resourceful in matters like this, despite all the emphasis on cloak-and-dagger stuff.

He continued on and the walkway extended into a huge area with several baggage carousels placed in consecutive order. Both the floor and walls were metallic gray, broken only by arcing patterns of black tiles on the floor. The ceiling arched upward, periodically supported by large silver pillars that ascended from the highly polished floors. Large blue signs with white lettering in both English and Chinese pointed the way to baggage claim and beyond that Arrival Hall A and all ground and rail transportation.

A pretty Asian woman in a blue police uniform stood holding a shiny weapon fastened to a strap running across her shoulder. It was a 9 mm JS submachine gun, the Chinese version of the Heckler & Koch MP-5. She also had a holstered semi-automatic pistol on one hip and a Taser stun gun on the other. She glanced at Bolan and gave him a welcoming smile.

About thirty feet away, as the walkway fanned out and gave way to an even more expansive area, the soldier caught a glimpse of a man in a gray suit standing next to a huge metallic statue. The statute itself looked like a cross between a corkscrew and an anchor. Bolan paid it little mind. The man, however, did get his attention. He was tall with longish brown hair and a medium build. The two other things of interest were that he was Caucasian and holding a sign that had Matt Cooper printed on it in solid black letters.

Bolan moved toward the man, tempted to just introduce himself and dispense with the password protocol that Brognola had told him about. Obviously, if the man had his name, he had to have been expecting him. But he was on foreign turf and needed the assistance of MI-6 to get things rolling. Best not to ruffle any feathers this early in the game.

The quicker the better, he thought. Bolan sized the guy up as he got closer. Maybe thirty-five, about three or four inches shorter than he was, with a wiry build. The slight bulge on the left side of his jacket told the soldier that the guy was probably wearing a shoulder holster. He stopped in front of the man, tapped the sign once with his index finger and said, "Can you take me to Winthrop Harbor?"

The man smiled. "By plane, train or automobile."

Bolan extended his hand. The man looked at it, then shook. That fit, too. Bolan knew the Brits didn't like to shake hands as much as Americans.

"A pleasure to meet you, Mr. Cooper," the man said. "Arthur Simmons. Do you have any bags?"

Bolan shook his head and pointed to his carry-on. "I travel light."

"Ah, splendid." Simmons flashed a smile and dumped the sign into a trash can. "Do come along. I have a car waiting."

Bolan did a quick survey of the area. No one else seemed to be paying them much attention. So far things seemed to be proceeding without a hitch.

Simmons was walking a few steps ahead of him. The Brit took out a cell phone and hit one of the buttons. After a few moments he said, "We're coming out to the car now." He listened, then said something Bolan couldn't make out and flipped the phone closed. Simmons looked back.

"Do excuse the phone call, but my boss is most eager to meet with you, Mr. Cooper." His smile radiated. "Most eager."

Bolan assessed the bulge again as Simmons turned. It looked a bit too large to be the standard-issue Walther PPK that most MI-6 agents wore. More like a full-size nine millimeter. Maybe things had gotten worse in Hong Kong since his last visit.

EDDIE LEE PLACED his cell phone back in the case on his belt and watched as the headlights from the limousine wound their way up the curving road. Beyond him the lights of Hong Kong glowed brightly, like shining jewels set against the black velvet of the sky and the dark water. The limousine drew closer.

Lee almost resented his uncle's insistence to meet at this remote mountain precipice overlooking the harbor. Still, it did assure both of them that no one could listen in on their conversation or spy on them.

The general was becoming more and more paranoid of late. But with stakes as high as this Lee could hardly blame him. Hopefully he would be able to set the next step of this deal into motion while Simmons and Wang Sze interrogated the American. Lee needed to know exactly what they knew. If only he could have interrogated Rossi before he died. Wang Sze had been too reckless, but hopefully this new agent would give them the information they needed.

The limousine pulled to a stop about thirty feet away. The lights were shut off but the engine kept running. The rear window lowered with electronic ease, and Lee saw the face of his uncle's number-one bodyguard, Chow Ming Ho. Chow had the rank of colonel, but Lee had seldom seen him in uniform. He figured Dear Uncle Yu would not be in uniform, either. Both men usually reserved these trips to Hong Kong as a mixture of business and subsequent pleasure. And Lee had lined up a group of beautiful girls to service them after this meeting was concluded. Keeping the general happy was paramount to his overall plan.

Chow stepped out in front of the limo and glanced around, bringing a laser-guided thermal sensor to his face. The bodyguard did a complete circle, reading the device as he turned. When he completed the 360 degrees, he grunted in satisfaction and nodded to Lee.

Lee nodded back.

The rear window lowered again and Yu stuck his hand out, palm down, and waggled his fingers, the Chinese gesture for Lee to come forward.

Lee walked over to the car and the door popped open.

"Come in, nephew," General Yu said. "It is good to see you."

Lee bowed quickly and slipped inside the limousine. It was spacious, with seats along the sides and a wet bar behind the driver's compartment. General Yu smiled, showing his gold-lined front teeth. The trace of enamel that remained had turned dark and was mostly worn away. Perhaps after this big payday his uncle could afford to get some new teeth. Or maybe he'd continue to emulate Mao and Deng and the rest of the old guard from whence he'd come, back in the revolution and stick with the rotting stumps.

"And to you, dear Uncle," Lee said.

General Yu held a glass toward him. It was small and filled to the brim with some kind of amber liquid. Lee knew he was bound by protocol to drink some, even though he preferred to keep a clear head during these meetings. He accepted the glass with both hands and brought it to his lips, barely letting them touch the liquid before bringing the cup down.

General Yu's brow furrowed. "You do not partake. Why?"

Lee bowed his head with a quick jerk. "I have much on my mind. The Arab is proving most difficult to deal with."

General Yu considered that, smiled and brought his own glass to his lips, drinking deeply. "They trust no one outside their faith. And even within they have many rivalries." He took another drink and squinted at Lee. "What was so urgent that we had to meet tonight?"

"Shahkhia is refusing to complete the money transfers until I can deliver the Sleeping Dragons to him."

The general's head jerked at the mention of the "Sleeping Dragons." He shook his head slowly. "Nephew, I have told you there is much risk involved in that. I cannot afford to move too quickly. You must have patience."

Lee felt the anger burning in his gut. This old fool didn't understand the pressure he was under. "Patience is a luxury. One that I don't have time for in recent days."

The corners of the general's mouth twisted downward. "Even though China is not bound by the ridiculous rulings of the Australia Group, we are still bound by the Chinese Weapons Convention." Yu set his drink on the shelf beside him and used his forefinger for emphasis. "I have already told you, it is much too dangerous if a weapon such as the Sleeping Dragons is sold on the black market."

Lee said nothing. Let the old fool rant a bit, he thought.

"Do you realize the risk I took letting you take those Pegasus drones?" Yu continued. "Those alone were a major undertaking."

"The drones without the gas get us nothing," Lee said. "I told you, we are dealing with a fanatic here. Rightly so, he knows the drones are useless without the Dragons."

General Yu frowned, said nothing.

Lee knew he had to exploit the man's weakness. He smiled. "Remember, this is a client who will make it worth both of our whiles. The payment will make your military pension seem like a pittance."

"But I must never do anything that would bring dishonor to the People's Republic," Yu said.

Lee glanced at his watch. It was after nine. He felt like saying, "Save your mindless, patriot harpings for the uneducated masses," but instead tried a more circumvented tactic. "Uncle, with what we will be getting paid, neither of us will ever have to work again." He flashed his most crafty smile. "And tonight I have some of the most exquisite delights for your sampling, imported directly from Taipei and Seoul."

At the mention of Seoul the general's eyebrows shot up. "Korean girls? I must admit, it has been a long time since I dabbled in those fineries. And Taipei, too."

Lee smiled. He had him now, like a fish swimming after the worm. "Did I fail to mention that I also had a European?"

Yu's eyes opened wider. "Oh?"

"A Russian. Beautiful red hair, exquisite white skin."

The general grinned lasciviously. "Nephew, you have outdone yourself."

Lee ducked his head with another quick bow of respect. He hated being obsequious, catering to this old, lecherous fool's prurient interests, but such was the price of ultimate success.

"I need the Sleeping Dragons in the next few days," he said. "I must have them to complete this deal so Shahkhia will fulfill his part and make the payment."

General Yu was staring off into space, obviously already dreaming of the riches and the pleasures of the flesh that awaited him. His lips pulled into a tight line and he nodded.

"I shall, of course," Lee continued, "not deliver the Dragons until the payment is complete. For both of us."

"It shall be done, nephew. It shall be done."

Lee's own mouth felt tight and dry, but he knew if he kept the old fool happy this night he would deliver the Sleeping Dragons as he promised. The general was nothing if not predictable. He glanced at his watch again: 9:25. Simmons was hopefully delivering the American to Wang Sze as they sat here. It was, as Lee so often said, just like playing *weiqi*. Or, perhaps using a more apt metaphor, he recalled the juggler from his youth. Only this time, instead of juggling colored balls or fruit, he was using sharpened meat cleavers.

JILLIAN DANSER WATCHED as the last group of passengers descended on the escalator. Not an Occidental in the bunch. Where the hell was this bloody American, Matthew Cooper? she wondered. She flipped the handwritten sign with his name against her palm a few times in the vague hope that one of the Asians strolling past her might suddenly stop and say, "I know I don't look it, but I'm Matt Cooper."

No such luck.

At the most, they cast amusing glances at her, nothing more.

Damn, she thought as the last group went by her. She put the sign under her rapidly moistening armpit and took out her mobile. Cleeves answered on the third ring.

"Do tell me you have some good news," he said.

"Sir, I'm afraid I don't. I've been waiting here for the longest time."

She heard Cleeves sigh. "Oh, dear me."

"Have you checked the flight information I gave you?"

"Yes, sir. The flight arrived on time thirty minutes ago."

"Do tell?" She could almost see Cleeves biting his lip. "I must look into this. I'm going to ring off and recheck my details. I'll call you back."

With that, Danser flipped her cell phone closed and began walking toward the main assembly area. Perhaps if Cleeves had seen fit to give her the right flight information earlier she could have checked to see if it had been delayed. But he would have checked on that himself, wouldn't he? He was probably double checking the information now, while listening, no doubt, to his favorite royal marching music.

Danser sighed. Her seemingly simple field assignment, collecting a man at the airport, had turned into a botched debacle. She walked past the twisted metal abstraction that she thought somehow passed for a piece of artwork and hoped that perhaps it was only a minor glitch or something. Perhaps the man's flight had been delayed and he would be walking through the gate shortly. In any case, she wouldn't know until Cleeves got back to her.

She took a deep breath and tried to reclaim whatever vestiges of optimism she could. After all, on something as simple as this, picking up an American getting off a plane, nothing could possibly be wrong, could it?

After about forty-five minutes of travel, Bolan began to notice the lights of the city getting brighter as they finally got into the New Territories and approached the Victoria Tunnel. Simmons, who had been chatting with someone on his cell phone, ended the call and smiled as they went underground.

"No reception down here," he said and slipped it into his pocket. "You have a cell phone?"

Bolan said nothing. The man had seemed glib when they'd first gotten into the car, asking a few questions about Bolan's trip and plans. When the soldier didn't answer, Simmons said, "I say, are you hearing me all right?"

Bolan nodded and pointed toward the shadow of the driver's head showing through the translucent privacy screen.

Simmons nodded and smiled. "Oh, quite."

That had ended his garrulousness, at least as far as it being directed toward Bolan. Ever since they'd left the airport Simmons had been on his cell phone constantly, which seemed to net little in the way of information other than to give periodic updates on their position.

For an MI-6 agent this guy was kind of a blabbermouth.

Loose lips sink ships, Bolan thought. He hoped the guy's supervisor would be more professional. It bothered him, too, that the Brits had gone to all the trouble of their little password exercise, and then sent a man who seemed to ignore basic protocol.

They emerged from the tunnel to a sea of colored neon lights and pairs of headlights zooming through the darkness in the opposite direction. Hong Kong was teeming, as usual, which was fine, but they seemed to be taking the long way around to the American Embassy.

Bolan decided to play dumb. "How much farther?"

"Not much longer now," Simmons said. He glanced out the window himself and turned back to Bolan. "My boss wants us to meet him in his favorite mahjong parlor and restaurant. He has a particular fondness for the takeout there." His quick grin flashed again. "I presume you're hungry after your long flight."

Bolan was, but didn't say so. Until he was reunited with his weapons, which were being transported by diplomatic pouch to the American Embassy, getting some authentic Chinese food was the last thing on his mind. The limo continued to jerk and stop as the traffic increased. Bolan didn't know exactly where they were, but saw that they were near the waterfront.

"I must say," Simmons continued, "for a Yank you are rather taciturn." He reached in his pocket and took out a pack of cigarettes, offering one to Bolan. "You don't mind if I smoke, do you?"

Bolan shook his head. He watched the man light up the cigarette and detected a slight tremor in his fingers. This guy was nervous. Not a good sign. The hairs on the back of Bolan's neck were beginning to tingle.

The car turned down a side street and came to a stop midblock.

"Well, here we are," Simmons said, smiling again. The tip of the cigarette glowed red. He removed it from between his lips and blew out a cloudy stream. "If you would be so kind." He pointed toward the door. The chauffeur had already scurried out and was pulling the door open.

Bolan climbed out of the limo and looked down at the

Chinese chauffeur who was standing there with a huge grin on his face. Simmons got out and tossed the cigarette into the gutter. The building was dark brick with a solid pair of wooden doors gracing the center. A rainbow canopy of rotating colored lights flashed overhead, and the large glass window read Wong Tu Do Mahjong, which was spelled out in English with bright red neon letters. Underneath were more twists of neon forming the Chinese characters. The soldier could see movement through the window, but little else. Simmons slapped a hand on Bolan's right shoulder and held his other palm out toward the door.

"You do like Chinese food, don't you?" he said as he gave Bolan a gentle push toward the door. "Do go in."

Bolan stopped and took out his sat phone.

"I need to check in first," he said. "You go ahead."

Simmons canted his head, his expression looking almost wounded. "Come on, old chum. Plenty of time to do that once we place our order."

His left hand pressed Bolan's shoulder with a little more force, but the soldier didn't move. He opened his phone.

Simmons sighed and took a step back, shaking his head. "You Yanks are a stubborn lot, aren't you?" His smile flashed for a moment then disappeared. He held out his left hand, palm up. "Do give me the phone."

Bolan glanced at the man's face, heard an ominous metallic snap and then looked downward. Simmons had flipped off the safety on a 9 mm Norinco Tokarev 213 pistol close to his side, pointed directly at Bolan's groin.

"The phone, if you please," Simmons repeated.

The soldier handed over his sat phone and nodded at the gun. "That doesn't look like standard MI-6 issue."

"Right again, Yank. Now do get your *arse* all the way in there." Simmons waggled the pistol toward the entrance.

The grinning Chinese chauffeur stepped around them and opened the door to the mahjong parlor.

Bolan stood still, evaluating his options.

"I don't like to repeat myself, so do go inside," Simmons said in his genial tone, then punctuated it with a more guttural, "Now."

As Bolan stepped through the doorway, he saw that the place was fairly well lit, with groups of men sitting around various tables playing mahjong and smoking. A red-velvet curtain hung on his left, and an ornately carved section of small wooden pillars was on the right. A series of ceiling fans slowly rotated, and small, folded paper figures looking like birds or dragons suspended on fishing wire oscillated in the hazy air. Two men were hunched over the counter by the cash register. Both looked up and one of them straightened. He was about six feet, but very broad and his arms sprang from a tight black T-shirt like half-gallon milk cartons. The man's face twisted into a smile and Bolan recognized the brutish features from the picture Hal Brognola had shown him earlier—Wang Sze, Eddie Lee's number-one enforcer.

"I'M TELLING YOU his flight arrived a full forty minutes before the time you gave me," Jillian Danser said into her cell phone. She paused, realizing her tone was a little too shrill than prudence would dictate. It was, after all, her supervisor on the line. "Sorry, sir. I didn't mean to sound so strident."

"Do tell?" Cleeves said. "What convinced you that he's not lost somewhere inside the airport? Perhaps he stopped in one of the restaurant bars for a quick one."

Danser took a deep breath before she started talking. "As I said, sir, that flight information was totally off. His plane landed at 2005, not 2115, and he was checked through customs at 2025. I'm with the police now reviewing the security footage. It's hard to tell, but it appears a man matching his description was picked up by another man, a Caucasian apparently, and they left the airport together at 2040."

"Oh, dear me," Cleeves said. "See what else you can find

out. I'd better check in with the Yanks on this. Let them know their man is missing. Call me on your cell phone if you find anything else."

"Will do, sir."

She heard Cleeves sigh. "I do hope this all has a happy ending."

So do I, Jillian thought. So do I.

BOLAN FELT SIMMONS shove him from behind. He had the Tokarev in his right hand. The soldier slowed his movements, taking two steps into the mahjong parlor, waiting for Simmons to get close again. This time Bolan felt the circular end of the barrel press against the small of his back. It was the move he'd been hoping for.

Pretending to take a step forward again with his left foot, Bolan instead pivoted, sweeping his right arm down and back. His forearm struck Simmons's right hand, knocking the weapon off to the left. Bolan continued his pivot, grabbing Simmons by the wrist with both hands and forcing the Tokarev upward and back. Simmons grunted in pain as Bolan swept his right leg back against the Englishman's calf in a perfectly executed judo throw. As Simmons fell backward, the soldier snatched the pistol from his grasp and brought the edge of the grip back across Simmons's face, tearing a large chunk of flesh from his cheek. The Chinese chauffeur lurched forward, both arms stretched toward the big American. Bolan pivoted again, this time using his fist to deliver a powerful uppercut to the Asian's jutting chin. His face twisted with the blow, which had obviously broken the man's jaw, and he crumpled to the floor.

Bolan whirled, catching a glimpse of the advancing Wang Sze and the other man who'd been behind the counter. The Executioner's left hand reached out to grab the folds of a thick red curtain suspended next to the doorway. He yanked hard on the fluffy material, feeling it pop loose from the securing hooks and come crashing down. The heavy folds of crimson velvet cascaded downward, covering Wang Sze and the other man like a parachute.

Bolan felt a shot whiz by his head. Perhaps twenty feet away another Chinese stood with his arm outstretched firing a semi-automatic pistol. Bolan instinctively ducked to his left, brought up the Tokarev and squeezed off two rounds. The Chinese jerked backward as the two projectiles punched him in the chest, leaving twin holes in the center of his light blue shirt.

Inside the club the mahjong players began to scramble away from the tables, running and shouting as the tiles and chips scattered. Bolan turned and saw the two men struggling under the velvet curtain. He delivered a swift front kick to the face of the one he assumed was Wang Sze, and brought the butt of the Tokarev down on the head of the other.

Another shot rang out, and Bolan saw a group of armed men suddenly advancing through the scrambling mahjong players. He raised the pistol and shot the lead man in the head. He collapsed to the floor and several of the men behind him tripped. Another man paused and brought up his pistol. Bolan's first shot stabbed into his chest. He noticed the Tokarev had a slight pull to the left and adjusted his aim, sending another round into the gunman's forehead. Two more of the mobsters shot at him, and the Executioner put a round in each one as he kept moving toward the doors. He got there just in time to meet Simmons, who was struggling to his feet holding his bloody cheek.

"Nice meeting you, too, old chum," Bolan said as he drove home a double left hook to the Englishman's gut and temple. The force of the blows drove Simmons through a section of wooden pillars like a runaway train.

Bolan turned and fired two more shots to slow any prospective assailants as his shoulder bounced against the doors. The slide locked back on the Tokarev.

Empty.

He pushed through the double doors and seconds later the hot night air hit his face and he was outside on the sidewalk. He shoved the gun into his waistband and sprinted to his left, figuring the natural tendency for the men chasing him would be to veer right.

It might buy me a few extra seconds, he thought. But only a few.

Behind him he heard the clatter of the doors being pushed open. Several men burst outside, yelling in Chinese.

Bolan sprinted halfway down the block when an alley appeared on his left. He veered into the dark area just as some bricks next to him chipped. Then he heard the crack of a shot. No lights and tons of rotting garbage overflowing from cans and garbage bins, Bolan reflected as he ran. It was as good a place as any for some escape and evasion, he figured, until he got about ten feet farther beyond the slight curve and realized the alley was a dead end.

Welcome to Hong Kong.

JACK GRIMALDI WAS completing the preflight checklist preparing for takeoff in the Learjet 85 XR when his sat phone rang. He glanced at the screen: Hal Brognola's number. He pressed the button and answered with a "What's up?"

"Where are you?" Brognola asked.

"Still in Osaka. Doing my preflight check. Why?"

"You hear from Striker?"

From the tone of his voice Grimaldi knew something was wrong. "Not since we parted company in Frisco. Why?"

Brognola sighed. "He's MIA. Missed the meet with MI-6 at Chek Lap Kok and the videotapes show him leaving with some guy nobody knows."

"How the hell did that happen?"

"I don't know. The Brits seemed like they took all the

right precautions. They even had a password set up and everything."

"Sounds like MI-6 sprung a leak." Grimaldi frowned. "Any idea where he is?"

"The GPS in his sat phone traced him to a mahjong parlor in Hong Kong. But he's not answering and now it went dead. I tagged the coordinates and shut it down. I'll have MI-6 check it out."

"That's not good."

"Yeah, tell me something I don't know." Brognola sighed again. "By the way, your equipment is waiting for you at the American Embassy. It was sent via diplomatic pouch."

Grimaldi tried for a positive spin. "I'm sure Striker will be glad to get his Beretta back."

"Yeah, let's hope so. How soon can you get there?"

Grimaldi glanced at the checklist and then his watch. "Almost ready to take off from here. If I push it, I can get there in under two hours."

"Don't push it too hard," Brognola said. "I want you to get there safely. I don't need two of you to worry about."

Grimaldi chuckled. "Yeah, well, I wouldn't be too worried about Striker if I were you. I imagine that whoever grabbed him is feeling like they got a tiger by the tail right about now."

BOLAN SPUN AROUND the curve of the alley and did a quick assessment. Lots of stacked boxes, overflowing garbage cans and heavy metal garbage bins. The lighting was dim at best, and most of the buildings had stairs leading down to solid-looking doors. He didn't have time to look for one that was unlocked and kicking a door in would leave a distinct trail. Instead, he stopped running and crouched on the far side of one of the large metal garbage bins.

The Tokarev was empty, and he had no extra magazine. It was useless except as a club, and the soldier wanted his hands free. He set it on the ground. A scurrying sound caught his attention and a huge rat shot past his fingers with a flickering squeal. A bottle rolled out from under the garbage bin in the rat's wake.

Now this is something I can use, Bolan thought, picking up the bottle by the neck.

He heard voices and fast footfalls coming his way, and noted more scurrying under the garbage bin to his left. Apparently his pursuers weren't the only Hong Kong rats that traveled in groups. Perhaps the Tokarev could be of some use, after all, if he could time it right. Holding the bottle in his right hand, he put his fingertips against the butt of the pistol and got ready.

The voices got louder, and two men came around the corner whispering in Chinese, semi-automatic pistols held straight out in a two-handed grip.

Bolan waited a few more seconds until they were almost at his point of refuge, then gave the Tokarev a hard shove under the garbage bin. Several rats scurried from under it, running over the feet of the two advancing men. The man closer to the bin jumped and yelled something Bolan figured was Chinese for "Rats!" The other man grunted and looked down. Bolan rose and slammed the solid part of the bottle against the face of the closer man. The glass shattered and sent a spray of shards into the air. The Executioner pivoted and grabbed the man's outstretched arm, twisting the pistol from his grip. Before the second man could react Bolan sent a side kick smashing into his gut. The gunner windmilled backward, knocking over two garbage cans before stumbling to the ground.

Bolan brought the pistol around and shot him once in the forehead. The man's head jerked back as the blood poured out his ears and mixed with the garbage strewed across the alley.

More voices.

Bolan stooped and recovered the second man's weapon. Another Tokarev, but this one was a Type 54. No safety lever.

The first man's gun was a QSZ-92—it had a 15-round magazine. If they were fully loaded and not too depleted, Bolan figured he now had some firepower to throw back at the bad guys. He moved to the edge of the building, exposing as little of himself as possible while still being able to aim, and fired the Tokarev five times toward the advancing group. At least two men fell, and the others jumped behind whatever cans could afford them cover.

The soldier heard something in one of the cellars almost right next to him. A metal double door made a scraping sound as it opened outward and a quizzical, old Asian face peered out between the doors. Bolan fired two more rounds around the corner and vaulted over the metal railing on the side of the descending cellar stairs. The old man's eyes widened in shock as he tried to pull the door closed, but Bolan grabbed it and yanked it back open, the force pulling the man forward onto the ground. Pushing through the doorway, the Executioner stepped over the old man, grabbed him by the collar and belt, and lifted him from between the open doors. He set the old man to the side then whirled back, slamming the doors closed and pushing the metal latch in place to secure them. They were in a dingy storeroom of some sort with sacks of rice and cardboard boxes everywhere. Bolan nodded an apology to the fallen man and pushed one of the high stacks of rice bags over, blocking the door. He then ran toward the lighted doorway at the other end of the room.

This doorway opened into a medium-size kitchen. Three men in dark-colored clothes and soiled aprons shoved long strands of pasty noodles into several big steaming metal pots. Bolan noticed the slide on the Tokarev was locked back, indicating it was empty, so he tossed it into the nearest empty pot as he went by. The workers exchanged exclamations in Chinese but didn't interfere. He came to another doorway with a long curtain of beads and bamboo strips. Pausing to glance through the slits, Bolan surveyed the next room: tables, chairs and customers busy eating, drinking and talking loudly. No sign of any bad guys. Bolan glanced behind him and heard a pounding sound.

Time to make a timely exit, he thought as he stuck the QSZ-92 into his waistband on his left side and pulled his shirt over it. He pushed aside the curtain and strode through the restaurant at a quick but not hurried pace. He figured he already stood out enough being the only Caucasian in the room. Nobody seemed to pay much attention to him. He pushed open the front door of the establishment and did a quick glance up and down the street. He'd apparently come out on the next block over from the mahjong parlor. No sign of any bad guys yet. But "yet" was the operative word.

A big blue-and-white double-decker bus made its way up the street. Bolan moved to the curb and waited until the bus was almost on him. He reached out, grabbing the vertical metal pole adjacent to the rear exit of the vehicle and stepping up on the exposed edge of the bottom step. His other hand closed over the metal pole on the opposite side of the exit. The bus proceeded down the street, picking up speed as it went.

Bolan felt the rush of the wind beat his face and tried to flatten himself against the door as best he could. A few passengers inside the bus stared at him through the glass window. One yelled something, and Bolan caught a glimpse of the driver's face in the elongated sideview mirror. The man's face went from surprise to a scowl, and he immediately slowed the bus to a jerking stop.

Bolan figured they'd traveled at least a block from his point of egress from the party. He jumped down to the street and walked away. He saw a taxi approaching from the opposite direction and hailed it. The man slowed and stopped, his face split by a huge grin.

Bolan opened the back door of the cab and got in, slouching down.

"Where you wanna go, boss?" the cabbie asked.

"Anywhere out of here," Bolan said. "And fast. There's an extra tip in it for you."

"American, huh?" the cabbie said. "I hear you all real good tippers, huh?"

"As long as you get me out of here fast."

"Will do, boss." The cabbie's wide grin flashed in the rear-view mirror. "No problem."

Bolan leaned back in the shadow of the cab as they rolled by the restaurant. A group of about five men was standing out in front of the lighted exterior, and Bolan identified one of them as Wang Sze. The powerful Chinese glanced up and down the street, shouting orders at the others. He lashed out with a quick back-fist, knocking one of the men next to him off his feet. The others scattered like the rats had in the alley.

Yeah, Bolan thought. Welcome to Hong Kong, all right.

Eddie Lee sat in the darkened room and watched the three figures intertwined on the bed through the one-way glass mirror. He knew that the video camera was recording all of his dear uncle's actions as he engaged in various sex acts with the two women. The Russian and the Korean were a perfect interracial complement—one Occidental and one Oriental. Not that the sight of the old man's pathetic performance titillated Lee in any way. It was only a matter of insurance, some leverage in case he might need it down the road. Even though Yu was family, Lee didn't fully trust his avaricious uncle. That's why he always made sure the video recording equipment was in perfect working order, but discreetly handled. He'd even had one of the best camera operators in Hong Kong at his disposal, operating the zoom lens to make sure his dear uncle's face was completely visible throughout his little encounter. The camera operator's silence and discretion were assured not only by lucrative payment, but also by the threat of a horrible death in case of betrayal. The wages of treachery are death, Lee often said.

General Yu fell back on the bed in exhaustion. The two women looked at each other with amused yet bored expressions. They'd earned their break, apparently.

Lee didn't begrudge the old man his carnal pleasures. Each to his own. Lee actually hoped he would never have to use the various videos of Yu's indiscretions in his bargaining with the man, but he had to anticipate and prepare for every eventuality.

His cell phone vibrated. Lee glanced at the screen, figuring it had to be Mustapha Shahkhia anxious about any progress in obtaining the Sleeping Dragons. But instead Lee saw it was Wang Sze.

He stepped away from the one-way glass mirror and gestured to the camera operator to continue recording.

Lee slipped out of the darkened room and passed through the next one. He went into the hall and walked down to the hotel balcony and stepped outside, feeling the cool evening air on his face. The cell phone continued to vibrate. He flipped it open.

"Boss," Wang Sze said. "We've got a problem."

"Oh?" This was not what Lee wanted to hear. He waited for the other man to continue.

"The American," Wang Sze said. "He got away."

"What?" Lee felt his anger welling up. "How in the hell…?"

"Sorry, boss. He took the gun away from Simmons and shot up the place. A couple of the boys are dead."

Lee considered that. A simple operation, or what he'd assumed was a simple operation, had gone badly. Instead of being surrounded and taken, his metaphorical *weiqi* opponent had outflanked him and taken his pieces instead.

I underestimated this man, Lee thought. I won't let that happen again.

He looked out at the sea of lights that formed the lighted cityscape like no other in the world. So many lights… So much potential.

"Boss?" Wang Sze's voice echoed on the phone. The cell phone buzzed with another incoming call: Shahkhia. Shit.

"Clean things up and get out of there," Lee said. "I'll get back to you later."

He let the Libyan's call go to voice mail. Let the Arab keep sweating. He was used to it, Lee thought. The bastard lived in the desert. Right now Lee had another matter to check into. He pressed the buttons to gain access to his cell phone contact list and selected the number he wanted. Before he pressed it, though, he gazed out at the myriad lights again and thought about the American, this new player in the game.

Perhaps I now have a worthy opponent, after all, he thought.

WINSTON CLEEVES FINGERED the folded paper dragon as he flipped his cell phone closed and set it on his desk after concluding the conversation. He looked around his dingy little apartment. Not very many amenities, except for the latest communication gadgets and his bloody computer. The Service always saw to that, but little else. He sighed. Four more months to go until retirement. Not retirement, really. After thirty-five years of devoted service he was being put out to pasture. As far as they were concerned, he was supposed to look forward to leaving this dingy little apartment in Hong Kong in exchange for another, equally dingy little place somewhere in England, alone till the end of his days. At least he had his unexpected nest egg to fall back on. All that money and no place to spend it… Yet.

He sighed. Cleeves was going to miss the mahjong parlor, as well, but not the gambling debts he always incurred. He fingered the paper dragon again and marveled that something so simple as a piece of plain white paper could be fashioned into something so intricate. Fifteen folds, Lee had explained to him, turning the paper into the dragon. He'd found one sitting on top of his daily newspaper delivery two days before, and another one this morning. It was Lee's signal for Cleeves to call immediately on a prepaid, disposable cell phone. That meant two things: Lee wanted information and was willing to pay for it.

Eddie Lee had been very amenable with Cleeves about letting his debt ride, and even excusing large portions of it once Lee had found out Cleeves was in the Service. The most recent favor involved an American coming to investigate the Rossi affair.

Cleeves had figured the Yanks were sending some CIA bureaucrat, a bean counter who would examine the Rossi matter with typical civil service boorishness and report back to Washington to await further instructions. Certainly not someone who turned out to be capable of handling himself in a firefight. Having just arrived, the man shouldn't have even been in possession of any weapons.

What was this world coming to when you couldn't even count on American circumspection and lack of resourcefulness in the Chinese dragon's backyard?

Cooper. Matt Cooper, Cleeves thought. The name did nothing to stimulate his cognitive recollection. He'd never heard of the man before.

Cleeves pressed the button on his compact disk player and turned up the rousing rendition of "The British Grenadiers" by the Cheshire Regiment. The good old-fashioned marching music brought him back to those halcyon days of yore, when the sun never set on the Empire, before they lost India, Africa and eventually the pearl of the Orient itself, Hong Kong. Thirty-five years of service…thirty-five years of negligible accomplishments.

But thank God we still have the Falkland Islands, he thought with a smirk. I almost landed on the wrong side of an Argentine prison during that debacle. Fighting the Iron Lady's war over a few stony hills and some sheep. Still, it had been a measurable victory. Perhaps our last one.

He dreamed whimsically about the days when being an MI-6 operative had meant constant danger and doing his government's important work. *On Her Majesty's Secret Service.* Good old Ian Fleming had enthralled a generation, all right. But he'd also sown the seeds of destruction as the entire world eventually began to believe all the celluloid glitz that was guaranteed to please American audiences who thought that MI-6 was all glamour and superspies.

Rubbish, Cleeves thought.

The Service was composed of dedicated individuals, much like him, who did the small, dirty jobs in the back alleys everywhere for inadequate pay and few benefits.

The benefits… Twenty-four months ago he'd come to realize just how inadequate the pay had been, and how slight the benefits were, that he had nothing much to look forward to when he returned to England and that minuscule pension check. And all that after being the Service's number-one man in Hong Kong for the past twenty years. Twenty years without so much as a slipup. So when Eddie Lee had handed him that first folded paper dragon and outlined the proposal of their association for mutual benefit, how could he have said no?

The rousing instrumental was reaching its crescendo, and Cleeves raised his arms to direct an imaginary orchestra through the climax.

His cell phone buzzed again, just as the music reached its final, christening pitch.

Danser again, damn her. She was taking this job way too seriously. As seriously as he once had. Cleeves lowered his arms and sighed, thinking he'd best answer it. The poor girl was probably out of her mind with worry that she'd screwed up yet another simple assignment. Plus, he still had to check back with the Americans about their missing man.

Whatever was this world coming to? he wondered as he picked up his cell phone again.

GRIMALDI HAD FINISHED securing the Learjet and signed the papers acknowledging the amount for storage fees. He paused to take one more look at the plane before he left. She was a beauty, all right. Sixty-eight feet of sleek black metal that flew with the grace of an eagle. The flight had been as smooth as rubbing satin over glass, the controls responding to his every touch, like a familiar lover. Aaron Kurtzman had done a great job setting this one up for him. Grimaldi made a mental note to tell him he'd outdone himself.

Judging from what Brognola had told him in Japan, Grimaldi figured that somehow the bad guys had intercepted the information about their mission and beat MI-6 to the meet. They'd obviously pulled off some kind of ruse and managed to grab Bolan. But grabbing the man and holding him were two very different things. He'd been with Bolan on too many missions, seen him in action too many times to feel anything but pity for his captors. That was, of course, assuming that the soldier had quickly seen through the subterfuge before it was too late.

Too late? Not likely.

Still, the slight, residual concern lingered as he walked through the isolated hallway toward the main terminal area. He came to one of those moving walkways and stepped on as he took out his sat phone and called Hal Brognola.

The big Fed answered on the second ring.

"Just checking in for a sitrep," Girmaldi said. "Any word on our prodigal son?"

"Negative," Brognola said.

Grimaldi caught the undertone of worry in the one-word response. Not that Brognola was prone toward being talkative even in the best of times. But Grimaldi knew the man vicariously sweated through each mission as if he were there.

"Tell Aaron the plane's a real sweetheart," Grimaldi said, trying to lighten the mood. "She flies as smooth as a date with a new girlfriend."

"I'm sure he'll be thrilled," Brognola said. "I heard from MI-6. They offered one of those profuse British apologies and are looking into what happened. They assured me they'd definitely be waiting for you at the gate this time."

"Really? They give you a new password, too?"

Brognola barked a laugh. Grimaldi figured he probably spit

out a piece of chewed cigar. "There's supposed to be a pair of male and female agents there. Jillian Danser and Winston Cleeves. Cleeves is their top man in Hong Kong."

"What am I supposed to do," Grimaldi said, "ask for their IDs?"

"Nah, I already raised hell with them over what happened to Striker, so they sent me their pictures." Brognola emitted a low growl. "Check your smartphone."

"Roger that." Grimaldi powered up his smartphone and as the screen came to life he saw a notification that he had one new message. He pressed the button to view it. Head shots of a man and a woman came into focus. The woman was attractive. Even features, long, dark hair parted in the middle.

Pretty, but no Celise Boyer, he thought. But I couldn't be so lucky.

The man's picture showed someone much older, overweight, and more than just a little shopworn.

No wonder he's their number-one man here, Grimaldi thought. He's probably been here since the eighties.

"Get them?" Brognola asked.

"Got them," Grimaldi said. "Thanks."

"Don't mention it. Now stay out of trouble and call me if you meet up with Striker."

"You mean 'when' I meet up with him," Grimaldi said. "Roger wilco."

He terminated the call and studied the pictures a few moments more while he coasted on the long walkway. When he was satisfied he'd committed the faces to memory, he deleted the pictures and replaced the smartphone in its case. The moving walkway ended and Grimaldi got on another one, but this one was shorter. Chinese customs had already gone through the plane and his luggage, so all he had to do now was to go through the upcoming security checkpoint and he'd be loose in Hong Kong. Well, Hong Kong airport, more exactly. Grimaldi knew he still had an hour's ride to get to the city itself.

As he passed through the checkpoint, he took in his surroundings. It was after midnight, and the airport was mostly deserted. Two Chinese policemen in their blue uniforms and dark berets stood chatting as he passed. Each had a well-oiled submachine gun hanging from a strap around their shoulders. The guns looked like Heckler & Koch MP-5s, and Grimaldi wondered if the Chinese had actually worked a deal with H&K or had simply copied the design and produced their own version like they'd done with the Russian Makarovs and Tokarevs. Regardless, they looked very intimidating and very lethal. One of the Chinese cops eyed him as he passed, and Grimaldi gave him a pleasant smile.

Beyond the checkpoint the hallway opened into a massive area with a domed ceiling, solid-looking steel pillars and suspended blue directional signs with white lettering in both English and Chinese. Beside a few more roving police officers and airport workers, the whole place looked like a big empty ghost town. Grimaldi did see two people sitting in a row of seats about fifty yards away, however, and recognized them immediately from the pictures Brognola had sent. Cleeves and Danser. The woman sprang to her feet and started walking toward him. The ponderous Cleeves looked a little slower getting off his considerable behind, but rose nonetheless and began his waddling approach.

The British are coming, Grimaldi thought, wishing he had a horse like Paul Revere.

As they got closer, he noticed that the woman was prettier in person than her picture. But she was still no Celise Boyer. He sighed.

I'd better get my head back in the game, he thought, instead of dreaming about movie stars I'll never meet.

Then he caught a glimpse of movement farther down. A big, broad-shouldered guy with dark hair who had been leaning against one of the round, metallic pillars straightened and began walking with an all-too-familiar gait.

Grimaldi felt an automatic grin spread over his face. The Brits weren't the only ones here to meet him.

"Hello, I'm Jillian Danser," the woman said as she walked up to Grimaldi.

"Nice to meet you," he said, and kept walking.

She did a double take, turned and watched him go by.

Grimaldi approached the heavyset guy who'd stopped and held out his hand.

"I say, I'm Winston Cleeves. I do believe we were dispatched here to collect you, my good man."

"Nice to meet you, too," he said, and continued walking.

Grimaldi strode over to the big guy with the dark hair and held out his hand. The two men shook.

"Glad you could make it," Grimaldi said. "Where the hell you been? Hal's worried."

"Don't ask," Bolan said. "Let me use your phone."

Cleeves and Danser were walking up to them, and Grimaldi turned and cocked a thumb at Bolan. "My associate, Matt Cooper."

"Ah, the elusive Mr. Cooper," Cleeves said, a smile elevating his jowly face. "So sorry, I do believe we missed you the first time around."

"You weren't the only ones," Bolan said and held his open palm toward Grimaldi. "The phone, so I can check in."

Grimaldi handed it to him and watched with his lingering grin as Bolan walked away to make his call. Cleeves and Danser were watching, too.

"I say, he's a man of few words, isn't he?" Cleeves said.

"You got that right." Grimaldi looked over at Bolan who was engaged in a conversation on the sat phone, seeming as calm and unperturbed as if he was just ordering a pizza.

Yeah, he thought, the Executioner was here, all right.

“I assure you both that I will do my utmost to look into how this dreadful matter evolved,” Winston Cleeves was saying from the left front seat of the little car. Danser was driving, and Bolan and Grimaldi were both crammed into the back.

The limo had been much more comfortable, Bolan thought as they sped through the night. But hopefully this ride would be a bit safer.

“I did send a few messages on my computer,” Cleeves said, “as well as some texts on the cell phone. I must say that I never expected that Eddie Lee would have the capacity to hack into my communications like that.” He heaved a sigh. “Jillian, do schedule another sweep of our office and apartments for bugs.”

“Yes, sir,” the woman said. She seemed to be concentrating on the drive.

“Well,” Cleeves said, “given the lateness of the hour, I suppose the best course would be to get you two gents to your hotel, then we can get started bright and early—”

“Where’s Rossi’s body?” Bolan said.

Cleeves raised an eyebrow. “His body?”

Bolan stared at him.

“Well,” Cleeves continued after a beat, “I would assume it’s stored at the hospital morgue where he was pronounced dead.”

“Let’s go there,” Bolan said. “I want to see it.”

"Now? Do you realize it is close to one in the morning?"

"Nothing like an early start," Bolan stated.

"But aren't you tired after your long trip?"

"He doesn't have time to get tired," Grimaldi said.

"Rather." Cleeves's expression became rather dour. "I suppose if we must." He shifted in his seat and told Danser to drive to Hong Kong General Hospital. "At this ungodly hour it might be a bit ticklish to stop by your embassy for your equipment. We can divert to my apartment where I could give you some sort of…temporary armament. It might be prudent, considering what happened to you earlier, Mr. Cooper."

Bolan shook his head and lifted the left side of his jacket, exposing the butt of the pistol. "I got that covered for the moment."

THE HOSPITAL MORGUE was a pristine room composed of white ceramic tile walls framing an equally pristine green tile floor. Sandwiched in the middle of one of the white walls were five rows of vertically stacked metal drawers, four to a stack, recessed into a shiny stainless-steel rectangular section. The attendant, who looked as though he'd been awakened from an unpleasant dream, led Bolan, Grimaldi, Cleeves and Danser to the third metal drawer from the right. The attendant checked his clipboard, the number on the drawer, and then pulled it open. A black plastic bag containing the contours of a human body lay on the flat bottom of the drawer.

Bolan saw a tag with Chinese characters affixed to the zipper. Below the characters, *Rossi, Paul* was written in English. He reached over and pulled down the zipper. It moved stiffly at first, as if resisting being opened, then began to slide smoothly the farther down he pushed. Bolan spread the flaps of the body bag apart. The corpse looked pale and a bit shriveled. A Y-shaped cut ran from the corpse's throat to the groin. It had been stitched back together with thick black thread.

"What did they list as the cause of death?" Bolan asked the attendant.

The man's mouth pulled into a tight line as he flipped through the pages on his clipboard. "I'm sorry, sir. I don't have that information here."

"I do believe we have a copy of the report for you," Danser said. "I did read it over and seem to recall they attributed it to a broken neck."

Bolan nodded to Grimaldi who helped him lift the supine body and roll it over. The back of the neck showed the remnants of a dark bruise and misaligned bones. Bolan gently lowered Rossi's body back to its original resting place then scrutinized the rest of him.

"You say they found him in a car?" he asked.

"Yes," Cleeves replied. "He'd apparently run off the road and struck a tree."

"And he was dead when they found him?" Bolan asked.

"I believe so, yes," Cleeves said.

"Was it a British-style car?"

"I beg your pardon?"

"Which side was the steering wheel on?" Bolan asked.

"The proper side, of course," Cleeves said with a smile. "The right."

"Was he still behind the wheel?"

Cleeves raised his eyebrows and cast a glance toward Danser. "Jillian, I believe you were assigned to look over the official accident report. Do you recall anything specific to Mr. Cooper's questions?"

"I do believe he was," she said.

Bolan nodded and ran his fingers over the upper surface of Rossi's right leg. "Did you see this, Jack?"

Grimaldi leaned forward. "Yeah."

"What on earth are you two looking at?" Danser asked.

"See that reddish line there?" Grimaldi pointed to the right leg again.

Danser nodded.

"It's called postmortem lividity. Where the blood settles in the tissue after death."

The space between Danser's eyebrows furrowed. "And this shows…?"

"That he was lying on his right side for an extended period after he died," Grimaldi said. "Once the heart stops pumping, the blood descends due to the gravitational pull. And once it reaches the lowest point in the tissues, it stays there."

Danser's eyes widened. "Meaning if he was found in a sitting position, or even slumped over on the passenger side, the lividity wouldn't have shown up on the right side of his body."

"Exactly," Grimaldi said. "The right side is the wrong side, just like for steering wheels."

A trace of a smile graced Danser's lips.

"What exactly are you insinuating?" Cleeves asked.

"Paul Rossi died of a broken neck, all right," Bolan said. "But not from a car accident."

"Somebody planted him in that car," Grimaldi said.

"Obviously there was an autopsy." Bolan pointed to the Y-shaped cut. "But a cursory one."

"Yes," Cleeves said. "Since Great Britain's lease expired, Hong Kong has taken some enormous steps backward in some areas."

"So in other words," Grimaldi said, "it was a half-assed job?"

"Quite." Cleeves pursed his lips. "As I said, I'm afraid that such things as medical examinations have slipped a bit the past sixteen years or so. In the old days we jolly well would have caught that."

Bolan turned to the hospital attendant. "The American Embassy will be contacting you later this morning regarding taking charge of his body."

The attendant made a slight bow and scribbled something

on his clipboard. "It is the family's wish that he be returned to the United States?"

"Of course," Grimaldi said, his expression turning serious. "Rossi was a former U.S. Marine, and the Corps never leaves its dead behind."

8

Midmorning beams of sunlight streamed through the pock-marked windows of the abandoned warehouse's second story, dappling the square concrete floor with a smattering of bright flashes and irregular shadows. Eddie Lee watched as the two opponents stalked Wang Sze in the makeshift ring. The rest of the warehouse was abandoned except for the fighters and the small group of men sitting off to the side in a section of chairs. Lee's men guarded the entrance. Wang Sze gestured for the two men facing him to come forward. His immensely proportioned body glistened with perspiration. This was the third consecutive match he had fought that morning, having knocked out the other opponents so easily that this time he decided to take on two at a time.

The men wore no protective equipment, and Lee noticed that his number-one bodyguard/enforcer's body didn't have the same chiseled look to it as when he'd won the bodybuilding titles a few years ago. Was that a faint trace of fat around his waist? Perhaps life had become too easy for him. He did let the American slip through his fingers. But that was one of the reasons Lee had told him to be at the warehouse ready to fight this morning: a bit of atonement that would let Wang Sze exorcise his pent-up aggression. Despite the excess weight, he still looked monstrously formidable, still incredibly huge with rippling arms displaying disproportionately large biceps and triceps that wound downward into flecked bands on his steely, muscular forearms.

When Lee had commented about this lack of abdominal striation before the matches began, Wang Sze had only shrugged. The cutting definition, he explained, was only achievable through the various chemical injections immediately prior to the contests. It was about appearance rather than performance.

But Lee was concerned about both. He had purposely invited his client to the fights to inject a bit of intimidation into their relationship. He did not want Mustapha Shahkhia thinking of betrayal down the road, and seeing Wang Sze, and knowing he'd have to face the Herculean enforcer in any confrontation, was a good psychological inhibitor. The Libyan was already a bit testy over Lee's insistence he wear the disguise—a long-haired wig, sunglasses and a baseball cap. But, as he'd explained, it was necessary due to a new development.

Lee glanced over at Shahkhia and his huge bodyguard, Abdul Sultan. The man had size, but did he have the strength and skill to take on Wang Sze? Lee would have liked to have seen that matchup, but doubted that he would. His interest and association with the Arab was totally financial, a means to an end. An end meaning permanent financial security for Lee. Seeing whether Wang Sze could beat the Arab giant, even in a sporting match, would be counterproductive. Besides, Wang Sze was at his best when he was unhampered by any rules. Both Arabs seemed transfixed by the ongoing contest, and Lee returned his attention to it. Time to shake things up a bit. Give the Arab a subtle demonstration of who the big boss was.

"Are you going to stand there looking at each other," Lee yelled down at them, "or fight?"

The first man attacked Wang Sze with a roundhouse kick, which he blocked with his massive forearm. He danced nimbly away and at the same time brushed away a snapping front kick from the second opponent.

Both of them attempted to close in on him again, and this time Wang Sze dropped the closer man with a fast back-fist to the face. His second opponent moved forward, but Wang Sze pivoted and sent a spinning hook kick into the man's temple. He dropped as if he'd been poleaxed.

Wang Sze looked up at Eddie Lee and grinned. He knew he had to make up for letting the American get away by putting on a good show, but Lee wasn't really that upset about the previous night's debacle. It was, he thought, a good reminder to keep his head in the game.

"Your man has great skill," Shahkhia said, turning to Lee.

Lee smiled. "And your bodyguard has great size. He looks formidable, as well. Does he ever compete?"

"Compete?" Shahkhia's mouth twisted into a frown. "We have no time for such trivial pursuits. My country has been engaged in a civil war for the past two years. It is enough to know that Abdul would lay down his life for mine."

The giant Arab's head swiveled toward Lee.

"And he has killed many men not only with a gun, but with his *jambiya* and his bare hands, as well," Shahkhia said. "But I did not come here this morning to watch some fighting exhibition. And I told you I am not in a mood for games." He held up the wig, cap and sunglasses. "Now, what progress have you made? When can I get the final shipment?"

Lee turned and waved for Wang Sze to join him in the stands. He left the two prone bodies on the square concrete floor and walked toward the stairs.

"I apologize for the disguise, but there has been a new development," Lee said. "One that must be dealt with first."

"What?" The Libyan's face creased with sudden anger. "What kind of development?"

Lee waited for Wang Sze to join them. He watched as his man stepped up next to him. The giant Sultan got up and stood over Shahkhia. The two bodyguards stared at each other like two wary tigers. Lee held up his hand.

"The American who was eavesdropping on our conversation a few nights ago," he said. "Apparently he was able to get word back to his superiors before he was killed."

"But I thought you said you had taken care of that?"

"Appropriate steps were taken. His death was made to look like an accident."

"And now what has happened?"

"The Americans have sent some agents to look into things." Lee was able to read the anxiety on the Arab's face. These people were so predictable.

"Americans," Shahkhia said, spitting on the floor and driving his right fist into his left palm. "I hate them. They killed my father, and were responsible for the overthrow of my country's government." His eyes focused on Lee's face. "Tell me where they are and I will send Abdul to kill them." He straightened his fingers and dragged his hand across his throat, mimicking a cutting gesture.

Lee was amused by the man's gesticulations, but he knew these Arabs to be very animated conversationalists.

"I assure you, the matter is being taken care of," he said. "There is no need for you to become involved in anything here in Hong Kong."

The Libyan pressed his lips together then let out an expectorant breath. "I must have more than assurances. Do you know how their NATO air strikes devastated us during the initial conflict?"

Lee gave him a reassuring nod. "Have you ever played *weiqi?*"

Shahkhia's frown deepened. "Played what?"

"Weiqi," Lee said. "I believe in the West it is called Go."

The Arab shook his head, his expression shifting from total anger to confusion.

"It is a game we have played here in China for centuries,"

Lee said. "It teaches one patience and strategy. Much like the game of chess."

"You don't need to lecture me on chess or tactics. My father, who was the Great Leader, sent me to the finest military schools."

"I know that," Lee said. "And I also know how pressing this matter is for you. But you must remember, in all conflicts patience and strategy will triumph."

Shahkhia considered that for a moment, then nodded curtly. "Very well. I will leave the Americans to you," he said. "For now. What progress have you made in obtaining the Sleeping Dragons?"

Lee paused as he glanced around. The Arab's brashness and tendency to speak carelessly bothered him, but the rest of Lee's crew had given them the customary wide berth of privacy so he wasn't overly concerned. He was glad that he'd chosen this empty warehouse site for their meeting though.

"As I told you before," Lee said, speaking slowly, "I am in the process of obtaining the Sleeping Dragons, but you must understand that such a weapon is closely monitored and heavily guarded. I must move very carefully."

"My people are battling the National Transitional Council puppets with virtually nothing. I need more than halfhearted attempts to take back towns with sporadic drive-by shootings. If I'm going to take back my country, I must be able to unite all the different tribes, the Bedarian, the Warfalla… We must all band together and strike, and to do that I need a significant and devastating victory. A rallying point."

"Which the drones and the Sleeping Dragons will give to you," Lee said. "Remember, these drones are specially adapted for this particular disbursement task."

"But I still need to assemble and learn how to use them," the Libyan said, his voice rising again. "Where are the technicians you promised me to arm and pilot the drones?"

Lee placed what he thought would be a calming hand on

Shahkhia's forearm, but the Arab jerked back as if he'd been slapped.

"The sheikh shall not be touched," Sultan said. He moved his huge body a step closer and doubled his massive hands into fists.

Wang Sze stepped closer, balling up his fists, as well. Although a full head shorter than the big Arab, his shoulders were just as wide, his stare just as determined. They looked like two powerful water buffalo staring at each other over a waterhole.

Lee appreciated the face-off for a few seconds and then laughed to break the tension. "Haven't we got enough problems dealing with our enemies to be quarreling over trivialities?"

The tension seemed to hang in the air for a few moments more, then dissipated. Shahkhia raised his hand and snapped his fingers. Sultan relaxed, his hands uncurling. Wang Sze waited a beat and then did the same.

It's all in using the appropriate strategy, Lee thought. Not making your move until you've set all your pieces in place.

"Rest assured," he said, "the matter with the Americans will be properly dealt with. I've already set some things into motion."

He saw the Libyan's eyes lock on his own and they stared at each other again, neither one speaking, neither one daring to blink.

"The Americans will be dealt with shortly," Lee said.

Finally, Shahkhia said, "For your sake, they had better be."

Lee held the Arab's gaze a moment more, then purposely let a sly smile creep over his lips.

"Trust me," he said.

"YEAH, TRUST IS AN elusive commodity these days," Grimaldi said as he yawned.

"So is sleep," Bolan said, slipping off his jacket and fitting his muscular arms through the straps of a shoulder holster. "You get enough rest?"

Grimaldi grinned. "Do we ever?"

Both of them felt at ease in the comfort and security of the American Embassy stateroom. They'd taken a taxi there after grabbing a quick five hours of downtime at their hotel. A couple of "extended combat naps" Grimaldi had called them. But despite the respite, they were both still dog-tired.

Grimaldi yawned again.

"Hey, knock it off," Bolan said. "They say that's contagious." He slapped the loaded magazine into his Beretta 93-R and sent the slide forward, chambering the top 9 mm hollowpoint round in the magazine.

"Sorry. You were telling me you trust Cleeves and company about as far as you could throw them?"

"Not even that far." Bolan secured the 93-R in its shoulder holster, which had been specially modified to accommodate the extended sound suppressor affixed to the gun's barrel. "The guy who picked me up at the airport yesterday had all the moves. He knew my arrival time, the name I was using, even their damn password sequence."

"You mean, their extra-special, secret-squirrel password sequence?" Grimaldi added. He began sticking his belt through the loops of a plastic pancake holster.

Bolan tested the fit of the shoulder rig, practicing his draw a couple times. "Yeah. It all adds up to something being rotten in the state of Denmark."

"Denmark?" Grimaldi flashed a grin again. "How'd the Danes get mixed up in this? I thought we were talking about Brits?"

Bolan snorted. "I'm glad all this adversity and lack of sleep hasn't affected what passes as your sense of humor." Satisfied with the fit of the shoulder rig, he checked the two magazines for the Beretta. One was filled with more copper-jacketed hollowpoint rounds and the other had RBCD total fragmentation rounds. He slipped those into the holders on the right side of the shoulder holster and then picked up two more magazines. They were filled with needle-pointed armor-piercing rounds that would penetrate metal as easily as they would go through Kevlar. After securing the magaziness in the belt holder on his left side, Bolan picked up his jacket and slipped it on. "Like I said, I smell a rat in MI-6."

"Hal and I thought the same thing once we heard you were MIA," Grimaldi said. He chambered a round into his 9 mm SIG-Sauer P-226 and gave it an admiring look as he screwed on the sound suppressor. "I have it on good authority that this was the gun that got Osama bin Laden," he said, giving it a pat before pressing the decocking lever and reinserting a fresh magazine.

"They did in Osama with an H&K 416," Bolan said.

"Whatever," Grimaldi said as he pressed the SIG in the locking, plastic shell holster. "If it's good enough for SEAL Team Six, it's good enough for me."

"Goodness had nothing to do with it." Bolan grinned. "And I was hardly MIA, by the way."

"Just subjected to a little inconvenience?" Grimaldi got down on one knee and stuck a .38 snub-nose Smith & Wesson Chief's Special into a nylon holster on his right ankle.

"Yeah, but it was just enough inconvenience to piss me off." Bolan picked up a Cold Steel Espada folding knife and flipped it open to test the flexibility of the weapon. It had a five-and-a-half-inch blade and could be easily opened by flicking the metal disk on the upper portion of the blade. Once fully extended it almost had the length of a Ka-Bar fighting knife. He refolded it and clipped it inside his pants on his right flank. "I told Hal to have Aaron start some covert security checks on Cleeves and company."

"Damn straight," Grimaldi said, then shook his head. "Man, I hope that woman, Danser, isn't involved. She's kind of a looker."

Bolan zipped up his loose-fitting jacket and checked his image in the mirror. The garment was baggy enough to conceal any trace of the Beretta and the knife. "Yeah, well, just remember even though we're not out somewhere beating the bush, we're still in what we should consider hostile territory here. And the Brits have got a security breach so we're on our own until we get that located." He took out the small portable radio, connected the throat mike and earphone and clipped the device on his belt. He held the other one out toward Grimaldi. "Which is why we need to carry these."

He stopped when he saw Grimaldi's attention was intently focused on the large flat-screen that had been flickering away on mute. Bolan looked at the television and then shook his head as images of a scantily clad Celise Boyer flashed across the screen doing some acrobatic kicks as she fired a pistol with each hand.

Grimaldi had to have caught the reflection of the movement and glanced back at him. "That's *Peppermill*."

"Huh?"

"Peppermill," Grimaldi said with a grin. "Celise's latest movie."

Bolan frowned and shook his head again. "The only Peppermill I've ever heard of is a bar in Las Vegas."

Grimaldi shrugged and clipped a pouch with two extra magazines for his pistol onto his belt, his eyes still affixed to the flat-screen. As he put on his jacket, he tapped Bolan on the arm. "Hey, do you think I could order that one?"

"Order what?"

"Her movie. On our hotel TV."

"As long as you're the one who explains that little necessity to Hal when he gets the bill," Bolan said. "Here." He tossed the radio to Grimaldi, who caught it and stuck it in his pocket.

"We submit bills to Hal?" he asked incredously, adding, "Not going to be much of a range with these without a repeating tower to bounce the signal off."

"Yeah," Bolan said, "but we'll be able to communicate if we're relatively close. So they're better than nothing." He made a few gestures with his arms while his partner checked out how the jacket concealed his weapon.

Grimaldi gave him a thumbs-up, then turned and did some movements to let Bolan check him. "It really is a good movie. She plays this superspy on the run, tracking down a couple of rogue international arms dealers."

"Looking for pointers?" Bolan teased and gave Grimaldi an all-okay pat on the shoulder. "We've got our own arms dealer to track down, remember?"

"Yeah, but it's Celise Boyer." Grimaldi shifted himself inside his own bulky jacket a few more times, checking his reflection in the mirror, then turned to Bolan. "I mean, I can dream, can't I?"

"Only on your own time. And once again, don't forget what I said about hostile territory."

"Well, at least we're dressed for the party." Grimaldi gave his jacket another tug and checked himself one more time in the mirror. "How do I look?"

Bolan gave him an exaggerated scan, grinned and slapped his partner on the shoulder. "Good enough to take Celise Boyer to the Peppermill."

"TRUST ME, MY DEAR fellow," Cleeves said as they walked across a stone bridge in Victoria Park toward a bucolic pathway with effulgent trees and manicured hedges forming a mazelike design. Cleeves had suggested the park as a meeting place because he hadn't yet gotten his office swept for electronic listening devices.

"Is that who the park was named after?" Grimaldi asked, pointing to a huge bronze statue of a woman seated on a throne.

Cleeves smiled. "Yes. Our Queen Victoria."

“What do you call her for short?” Grimaldi asked. “Queen Vickie?”

Cleeves frowned. “‘Her Majesty’ was the customary title. She was on the throne when Britain first signed the lease with China after winning the opium war in 1897.”

“Are you sure this park was the best place for our meeting?” Bolan asked. “Looks like quite a few prying ears around here.”

“It’s also a place where we’ll fade into the crowd,” Cleeves said. “Quite a few of the local politicians often come here to extol their own virtues.”

“We call that blowing your own horn, in the States,” Grimaldi said.

“Quite.” Cleeves wiped a handkerchief over his forehead.

Bolan noticed the man appeared flushed from the mild exertion of walking over the incline. Or was he just nervous? Bolan glanced back at Grimaldi who was bringing up the rear. Off to their left, six men, led by an older Chinese in a white, Mandarin-collared jacket, were performing synchronized tai chi movements.

“You mentioned you were going to bring us up to speed on Eddie Lee,” Bolan said.

“I believe I did,” Cleeves said. “I’ve had my top man on a surveillance of him well before your arrival. We’ll collect his report shortly.”

“Any idea how they were able to intercept the password instructions?” Bolan asked. He watched Cleeves closely as he replied.

“I’m afraid Hong Kong isn’t quite as secure as it used to be back in the days when we were in charge.” Cleeves huffed a breath, and the walkway leveled out to a series of square concrete blocks that expanded into a wide sidewalk. They passed another group of Chinese, this one all females, performing more tai chi movements.

Grimaldi made a clucking sound. "Now that's more like it. I wouldn't mind attending a couple of those sessions."

Bolan shot him a hard stare. "Keep your focus."

"It is safe, I assure you," Cleeves said. They walked a few more steps past a three-foot-high statue of a dragon made out of white marble. "Would you describe again that chap who collected you?"

"White male, mid-thirties, longish hair," Bolan said. "Used the name Arthur Simmons."

"Ah," Cleeves said, a wry smile tracing over his lips. "The redoubtable Mr. Simmons. A rather bad lout and sorry excuse for an Englishman. The type whose ancestors should have been shipped off to Tasmania back in the 1850s."

"Tasmania?" Grimaldi said. "Wasn't that where Errol Flynn was from?"

Cleeves frowned. "It was originally used as a penal colony where undesirables were shipped from England."

"So you've heard of him?" Bolan asked.

"Simmons? Yes." Cleeves heaved a deep breath. "Unfortunately, as I said, he's a sorry excuse for an Englishman. And, he's former MI-6. Went rogue about seven years ago. That's, no doubt, how he knew about the password sequence."

"How would he know the exact wording?" Bolan said. "Isn't it changed each time?"

"Oh, most certainly." Cleeves was talking quickly now and his breathing had quickened. "I'm still in a bit of a tizzy over the prospect of Lee's group having hacked into my email accounts and such. But I am having the matter looked into most thoroughly."

Bolan considered the man's explanation as he surveyed the area. The sidewalk leading through this section of trees was dappled with sunlight. The Executioner saw two people sitting on a bench up ahead. One was a man and the other was a woman he recognized as Danser.

"What's this new guy's name?" Bolan asked. "The one who's been shadowing Lee."

"Hugh Fawkes." Cleeves smiled. "No relation to the infamous Guy Fawkes."

"Who's that?" Grimaldi asked.

Cleeves huffed a slight laugh. "Oh, dear me, I'd forgotten that you Americans are not well versed in proper history. Guy Fawkes was a bit of a radical back in 1605. Planned to blow up Parliament and assassinate King James I and replace him with a Catholic monarch."

"Sounds like some of the people we've dealt with," Grimaldi said. "What happened to him?"

"He was caught and about to be hanged when he committed suicide by leaping off the gallows and breaking his neck." Cleeves smiled pleasantly. "We celebrate the anniversary of his death each November fifth by burning him in effigy and setting off a display of fireworks."

"Sort of like our Fourth of July," Grimaldi said with a broad grin.

The smile faded from Cleeves's face. "Quite. There they are now."

Danser and the man with her stood and Bolan gave him a quick once-over. He looked trim and fit, in his late thirties, with blond hair combed back in a small, wavy pompadour. He was holding a large manila envelope. The man smiled as he extended his hand.

"You must be Mr. Cooper. Hugh Fawkes."

They shook and Cleeves introduced Grimaldi, as well, as they moved over to a hexagonal metal table surrounded by six circular seats. When they were settled, Cleeves took the initiative and asked Fawkes what he had to report.

"Nothing much in the way of surprises, I'm afraid, except for these." Fawkes unwound the string securing the flap of the envelope and slid out a sheaf of eight-by-ten photographs. The first one had a pinkish tint that suggested it had been shot through an infrared lens. The photographs were taken from a distance and the images were not totally distinct. They showed three Chinese men in suits entering what appeared to be a hotel. Bolan recognized one as Lee.

"This fellow is Eddie Lee, of course," Fawkes said, placing the tip of his capped pen on the photo. "This one is his uncle, Yu Chow Yoon. Yu's a general in the People's Liberation Army and Lee's main source for black-market weaponry. He's had quite a bit of success getting his little toys out of the country under the guise of a sham company he operates known as Hong Kong Imports-Exports Unlimited."

Bolan nodded. So far Fawkes hadn't told him much he didn't already know, but the soldier always listened to any and all information available.

Fawkes put the pen on the third Asian's head. "This individual is the general's bodyguard, Cho Ming Ho. He holds the rank of colonel and has a considerable reputation for both loyalty and ruthlessness."

"Where were they going?" Grimaldi asked.

"The InterContinental Hotel in Kowloon. Lee usually sets up his uncle's assignations with prostitutes there." Fawkes smiled. "My sources informed me that this particular evening was quite active."

"Pass the Viagra, eh?" Grimaldi said.

"Yes, quite," Fawkes said. "It all seems to indicate that Lee is in the process of setting up a major deal." He shuffled through the sheaf of photographs and produced one of two men, one extremely large, walking toward a pair of double doors that appeared to be a warehouse. Both men were wearing sunglasses and baseballs caps. Long tresses drooped from under the caps.

"These were taken earlier this morning at an old warehouse on the waterfront," Fawkes said. "Lee often holds some underground fighting matches there to keep his bodyguards in fighting shape." He shuffled through the photos some more. "This is Wang Sze, his number-one enforcer."

"I've seen him up close and personal," Bolan said. "He was at the mahjong parlor they forced me into."

"The Wong Tu Do parlor, no doubt," Fawkes said. "It's one of Lee's principal lairs. You should consider yourself quite lucky, old chap. Wang Sze is quite the formidable adversary. Not many men have encountered him and lived to tell about it."

"That's only because he hasn't tangled with us yet," Grimaldi said.

Bolan gave him a look that told him to cool it. "Any idea who those guys wearing the sunglasses and wigs are?"

Fawkes shook his head. "Definitely Occidental from the look of their noses. Possibly Mediterranean if I had to venture a guess. I requested the photos be sent in for identification review." He looked at Cleeves, who cleared his throat.

"Still waiting for news from the home office on that," Cleeves said.

"We'd like to run them through our computer facial recognition program, too," Bolan stated. "The sooner we can find out who they are, the quicker we can figure out what this is all about."

"I'll see to it," Cleeves replied.

"Where's Lee at now?" Bolan asked.

"He was at the hotel with his uncle, the last I heard," Danser said. "Our man Higgins is watching him."

"Let's plan on joining him soon," Bolan said. "You have any idea what 'Sleeping Dragons' means?"

Danser shook her head and glanced at Fawkes, who pursed his lips, thought for a moment, then shrugged. "Haven't the foggiest. Winston?"

Cleeves leaned forward and cleared his throat again as he got to his feet. "Doesn't ring any bells. What I will do is send those photos to your contact in the States forthwith.

And I'll also see if any of my private sources inside Hong Kong Imports-Exports Unlimited can tell me what Lee's got planned."

He fished in his pocket and took out his cell phone, but a folded piece of paper came out with the movement. It fluttered downward and landed on the tabletop. Bolan reached over and picked it up. It was a folded paper dragon.

"What's this?" he asked, looking at it before handing it back to Cleeves.

"Oh, it's nothing. Just a bit of idle tomfoolery." Cleeves grabbed the dragon and jammed it back into his pocket, holding up the cell phone in his other hand. "Excuse me while I make a few calls."

"We better check in, as well," Bolan said, taking out the sat phone he'd acquired at the embassy. He nodded at Grimaldi, and the two men stood and walked away.

"Going to give Aaron a heads-up on those photos?" Grimaldi asked when they were out of earshot of the Brits.

"That, and to tell him to concentrate his investigation of our MI-6 friends on Cleeves."

Grimaldi's eyebrows rose.

"I've seen one of those folded paper dragons before," Bolan said. "During my visit to the Wong Tu Do Mahjong parlor."

9

“What do you mean, the antenna is not yet complete?” Mustapha Shahkhia said menacingly into the hotel phone. “The first shipment of drones is already on its way there.”

The man on the other end of the call offered a thousand pardons. The Libyan could sense the fear in the man’s voice and that was good. Even though the lackey was thousands of kilometers away in Libya, the man knew Shahkhia’s influence could easily reach out and have him killed.

“It is almost completed, sir,” the man continued. “And I assure you we already have people waiting at the rendezvous place to meet the shipment and transport it immediately to our headquarters.”

“You had better. If all is not as it should be upon my return, you will scream for mercy and welcome death’s embrace.” He slammed the phone into the cradle.

Shahkhia mentally assessed the situation, considering all the contingencies as any smart military commander would do. The shipment of thirty-five Pegasus drones should be arriving in Egypt in about fifteen hours under the guise of medical supplies. From there his emissaries would intercept the shipment and take it to the desert base in Libya where the assembly would begin. That should take no longer than thirty-six hours.

All that remained would be the final completion of the antenna to convey the broadcast of the target coordinates to the computerized guidance systems. He frowned at the thought he would still need the Chinese technicians to program the initial strikes and arm the two separate portions of the Sleeping Dragons. But after that they would be expendable.

He thought of the NATO airpower and took into account again his need for more insurance against them after his first strike decimated the capital and the NTC puppets. The Americans would respond quickly, no doubt, after their usual bellicose rumbling in front of their television cameras, and most probably launch planes from one of their carriers that could destroy his forces in the blink of an eye. If and when they could find him, that was. As long as they could keep on the move after their first strike, with his army and the tribes in rebellion, it would buy him time. The Americans would eventually lose their will. He need only prevent their initial retaliation and he knew how to assure that.

He looked over at Sultan who sat patiently watching him. "Has the television been replaced?"

The huge man nodded and handed him the remote. Shahkhia took it and pressed the power button. The screen came to life and he shuffled through the menu until he found a worldwide cable news station.

"I'm looking for news about the whore of the West," he said. "She must be on her way to our country by now."

"Along with the other United Nations lackeys," Sultan said.

"Check with our sources inside the capital," Shahkhia said, continuing to flip through the channels. "Find out when they'll arrive and in which hotel they'll be staying. I want our capture of them to be as precise as slicing the throat of a lamb."

"It will be done, sir." Shahkhia watched the big man as he got to his feet. Sultan's devotion was one of the cornerstones of his assured success, and he wanted to make certain of his bodyguard's continued loyalty.

As luck would have it, the television channel suddenly displayed the figure of Celise Boyer in some kind of a movie advertisement. The woman was clad in a scanty outfit doing a martial arts kick while firing a pistol. The movement stopped and the picture centered on her face.

No woman but a whore would display herself in such a fashion, thought Shahkhia. Still, he noticed Sultan's eyes lock on the woman on the screen. Perhaps he could use her beauty as a motivator for his faithful guardian. It never hurt to capitalize when an opportunity presented itself.

"It is God's will that we keep the whore of the West and the rest of them with us to ensure the Americans will not strike at us," Shahkhia said. "But I shall place her in your personal custody to be your slave to do with what you want. You can instruct her in the proper ways of Islam and of a woman's place."

Sultan's eyes flickered for a moment as he watched the images on the television screen, obviously relishing the thoughts of such a fantasy. A beautiful and corrupt woman to do with as he wished, with no consequences. A smile crept over his lips.

Shahkhia glanced at his watch. It was close to the time of their next meeting with Lee. Hopefully the Chinese jackal would have news of the Sleeping Dragons. Then the final phase would begin.

EDDIE LEE BIT into his egg roll as he watched his dear uncle and his bodyguard leave the back entrance of the hotel. They got into the waiting limousine that would take them to the rendezvous point for their helicopter ride back to the Mainland. Uncle Yu had a smile of serenity on his face, as well he should. The chemical enhancements had done their job and his session with the two women had lasted well into the night. Lee smiled as he thought of Yu's expression should he view the tape. He imagined moving more white disks around his uncle's exposed flank of black pieces in a game of *weiqi*.

An easy victory. But he still had to deal with Shahkhia, and the impatient Arab was proving to be a more problematic opponent.

Lee's cell phone rang, and he glanced at the screen—Cleeves. He stepped out into the alleyway behind the hotel and answered it with a curt, "Hello?" Over his shoulder he could see that Wang Sze had followed but was maintaining the customary respectful distance.

"We may have a bit of a problem," the Englishman said. "The Americans might be close to identifying your new clients."

Lee had purposely kept Cleeves in the dark about the Arab's identity, saying only that he was dealing with a Middle Eastern entity. If the Americans identified Mustapha Shahkhia before the final fund transfer, the entire deal, and Lee's hope for total and complete financial independence for the rest of his life, could be in jeopardy. After the money had been transferred Lee couldn't care less if the Americans or their NATO surrogates destroyed the son of a bitch. It would even work out for the better, making it more difficult to trace the Sleeping Dragons back to him.

He moved a few more white disks on the imaginary board in his mind.

"Where are you now?" he asked.

"Victoria Park," Cleeves said. "And I've only got a bit of time. I'm supposed to be checking with a source on your whereabouts."

Lee considered that as he licked his lips. He stared at the egg roll in his hand but had suddenly lost his appetite. He tossed it behind some nearby garbage cans then glanced at his watch. In thirty minutes he was supposed to meet with Shahkhia. He didn't trust the Arab completely and wanted to take Wang Sze with him. Still, he needed someone competent to handle this new problem—more of a ripple in the pond, really.

"I have an idea." Lee gave Cleeves some quick directions and hung up.

He turned to Wang Sze. "Get hold of Simmons."

Wand Sze nodded and took out his cell phone.

Lee thought again about sending his number-one man to make sure the job was done right, but it was more important to have Wang Sze with him when he met the Arab. Besides, Simmons was still smarting from his ignominious first encounter with the American, Cooper. Perhaps it would give him some incentive to do the job right this time. He glanced at the departing limousine and had another thought. Perhaps his dcar unclc could provide him with a slight edge taking care of this problem. He flipped open his cell phone.

A sudden chirping and accompanying scurry to his right told him the rats had found the remnants of his egg roll. He knew the garbage can area of the alleyway was normally laced with heavy spring-loaded traps, and smiled as he heard a sudden whisk of sound accompanied by an abrupt squeal seconds later.

The trap had done its job, he thought. Excellent. Hopefully it would prove to be an appropriate omen, as well.

As the boat sailed across the bay, the green foliage of the mountainous region was broken by the sight of four distant buildings sandwiched between an outgrowth of high trees. The buildings were a dull yellow color and looked like cardboard detritus strewed among the plant life. Bolan stood in the pilot's station beside Grimaldi and Danser, watching the scene unfold in front of them as the salty mist speckled the windshield. Fawkes was at the wheel, and the steady hum of the twin Mercury inboard engines acted as a remote reminder of their steady progress across the choppy water. Bolan assessed the place.

A smaller, three-story building was closest to the beach and set perpendicular to three larger structures. Each one had the typical Oriental design—ornately peaked four-corner roofs jutting over a series of flourished balconies.

"Is that the place Cleeves told us about?" Bolan asked.

Fawkes, who was piloting the midsize yacht, nodded. "It's called the Imperial Palace, or at least it was at one time." He smiled. "The place has been abandoned for at least a year and a half. It went into foreclosure after the business fell off."

"Is this still Hong Kong?" Grimaldi asked.

"It is," Fawkes said. "Westerners often tend to think of Hong Kong as a city, but it's actually an archipelago—a series of islands. About two hundred and sixty of them to be exact. The fortunes of resorts like these come and go as often as the tides. It used to be quite the tourist attraction, and could hold over a thousand guests in its heyday."

"That's a lot of buildings to check out," Bolan said.

"According to Winston, the only one that's habitable is the one right off the walkway, and even that one's in a state of severe disrepair," Fawkes said. "The ones to the rear are purportedly overrun by birds and lizards."

"How about rats?" Grimaldi asked.

"Indubitably," Fawkes said.

Sounds like a nice place for an ambush, Bolan thought. He turned to Danser. "Your man Higgins still got an eyeball on Eddie Lee?"

She smiled slightly and nodded. "He shot me a text a few minutes ago. Lee's still at the harbor. How is it you Americans say it? Sitting at the dock of the bay?"

"Otis Redding," Grimaldi said. "His big, breakout hit. Also his last. He got killed just when it was released."

"A pity," Danser said.

Cleeves had assured them that his source had been most specific. Lee was bringing his mystery clients to the remote location for some sort of definitive demonstration. "It was supposed to seal the deal," Cleeves had said. "This could be a significant clue as to what Lee's been up to. The Imperial Palace is remote enough to provide a jolly good demonstration."

Or a jolly good ambush, Bolan thought again as he remembered the look on the Englishman's face. He asked Fawkes how much longer until they got there.

"We should be docking in no more than fifteen minutes," Fawkes said. He smiled as he piloted the vessel through the choppy water.

"You sail this thing pretty well," Grimaldi said.

"Thank you. Eight years in the Royal Navy before joining Her Majesty's secret service," Fawkes said.

"No kidding?" Grimaldi said. "How is the world's second-best navy doing these days?"

Fawkes smiled. "Funny, I was going to ask you the same question, old boy."

Bolan left the cabin and went to the back of the boat to use his sat phone to call Stony Man Farm. Brognola answered.

"I was figuring you'd call back," he said.

"You guys come up with anything yet?" Bolan asked.

"Not in the past forty minutes since your call."

"You check things out with MI-6?"

He heard Brognola sigh. "Like I told you, you'll have to give me more than just folded paper dragons and supposition if you want me to go yanking MI-6's chain about one of their senior agents. He's been in the service more than thirty years."

"That dragon and my intuition match up pretty well with that little reception party at the airport, don't they?" Bolan asked.

"Yeah, but I'll still need something solid," Brognola said. "Jack and I already figured there was a leak somewhere, and Aaron's been working around the clock unofficially looking into things."

"Good enough. Cleeves was supposed to be sending you some pictures to run through facial recognition, too. We need a quick turnaround on them."

"We'll get right on it. When we get them, that is, considering it's close to two in the morning back here."

Bolan chuckled. "What are you doing staying up so late?"

"Waiting for another sitrep from you, dammit," Brognola said. Bolan could almost see him chewing on one of his thick cigars. "In the meantime, you and Jack watch each other's backs, okay?"

"We're probably going to get a lot of practice shortly."

Grimaldi was descending the stairs from the captain's perch and coming toward him.

Bolan heard Brognola's sigh again. "Maybe it'd be better to back off until Aaron's finished checking everything out."

"Not with the clock ticking double-time."

"All right, but like I said, you two watch your six."

Bolan said they would and terminated the call.

"So what did Hal have to say?" Grimaldi asked.

"Just to watch our asses," Bolan said. "Asked if we wanted to back off for a bit."

Grimaldi snorted. "Like that's an option."

The syncopated sound of helicopter blades slicing the air grew louder and a craft flew overhead coming from the direction of the mountains behind the Imperial Palace.

"Looks like an AS 332 Puma," Grimaldi said, cupping his hand against his forehead as he looked at the sky. "Holds up to sixteen passengers with a crew of three."

Bolan watched as the helicopter continued on overhead then banked left toward the adjacent island and disappeared behind another slope of mountains. "You know, we could be walking into a trap."

"Tell me something I don't know." Grimaldi smirked. "But it's just like my old uncle Gordon used to say. When the other guy's holding all the aces, sometimes the only thing you can do is kick over the table."

EDDIE LEE SIPPED his drink and watched as Mustapha Shahkhia and his bodyguard approached the gangplank. The suspended walkway strained under the giant's weight, and Lee was amused at the thought of both Arabs falling into the dirty water beside the boat. But he pushed away his imagined amusement in favor of the consideration of his plan. It was one larger plan made up of several smaller ones, each like cogs turning a big wheel. He set the drink on the wet bar and picked up his phone to call Cleeves. The Englishman answered immediately, and Lee could hear marching music in the background. What a fool this man was, inspired by such repetitive monotony.

"Is everything still going according to our plan?" Lee asked.

"Quite," Cleeves said. "They should be arriving at the agreed-upon spot shortly. When they do, they'll check in with me and I'll call you back."

Lee did some mental calculations, figuring how long it would take Simmons and the others to arrive. Having the helicopter would give them the edge, no doubt, and with a squad of dear uncle's trained soldiers, the Americans should be no problem. He'd given the instructions to take at least one of the Americans alive, if possible, for interrogation. Lee hoped it would be the one who'd escaped the day before. A worthy adversary, he remembered thinking. Breaking such a man would not only be a challenge, but also an enjoyable experience.

"The two of your men and the two Americans, correct?" Lee asked. "No one else?"

"Four is correct," Cleeves said. "But one of mine is a young lady. Do make it as painless as possible for her, will you? I'd hate to think of the young thing suffering unduly."

Lee was unimpressed with Cleeves's request. The man had no true honor, not even the dubious integrity of a loyal thief.

When the time came, he thought, this one, too, should be eliminated without compunction.

"I shall see to it," Lee said. "I assume your man is still watching me here?"

"Of course," Cleeves said.

"Well, you should be hearing from him shortly. My guests have arrived and we will disembark."

He ended the call as Wang Sze ushered Shahkhia and the giant into the plush cabin.

"Would you care for a drink?" Lee asked, a crafty smile creeping over his lips.

The Libyan shook his head. "It is forbidden for us. You should know that."

"Of course," Lee said. "It is merely that I feel in a celebratory mood. One of our mutual problems is about to be eliminated."

"I SAY," FAWKES CALLED from the captain's perch. "Could one of you jump onto the dock and secure that line to the bulkhead?"

Grimaldi called out that he had it covered and grabbed the coil of rope and moved up to the front deck.

The concrete pier jutted from the blue water and seemed to get closer and closer as Bolan watched. The gears ground momentarily as Fawkes jammed them into Reverse to slow the boat's approach.

The Brit was good with boats, Bolan thought. He'd give him that. Now he just hoped he'd be equally adept at planting some cameras and listening devices and getting them the hell out of here before Lee and company arrived. Bolan turned to Danser, who was talking on her cell phone.

She flipped it closed and said, "Looks like Lee has his clients on board and is getting ready to shove off, but he's still at the dock."

"That gives us what, about fifty, sixty minutes tops?"

Danser nodded. "I would suppose."

"We'd better move it then," Bolan said and braced himself as the anchoring line pulled taut.

Grimaldi was on the concrete pier, scanning the walkway that led to the abandoned hotel. It was perhaps a hundred yards away and ran on top of a twelve-foot-high concrete wall perpendicular to the sandy beach.

A tide wall, Bolan thought. He moved to the side of the boat and picked up two duffel bags with the eavesdropping and recording equipment. Fawkes jumped onto the pier and smiled up at him.

"Very good of you to carry all that, old boy," he said with

a wide smile. "Are you planning on taking them the rest of the way up?"

Bolan jumped onto the pier next to Fawkes and set the bags down. "You carry them. My partner and I have to clear the area first. Stay here until we give you the all-clear. Probably be wise to find some cover in the meantime."

Fawkes raised both eyebrows. "I say, do you think all that's necessary? After all, our man Higgins said that Lee hasn't even left yet."

Bolan reached inside his jacket and withdrew his Beretta 93-R. Fawkes's eyes widened.

"Humor me," Bolan said as he secured his earphone and tapped Grimaldi on the shoulder. "Ready?"

Grimaldi was activating his own earpiece as he took out his SIG-Sauer P-226 and grinned. "I was born ready."

They began a quick trot toward the Imperial Palace. As they got closer, Bolan noticed the dilapidated state of the place. The yellowish paint of the building had faded to a dull tan, and the sidewalk was overgrown with weeds that cropped up through the cracks and splits in the concrete. The shrubbery on their right showed little sign of having been trimmed in several months, and the windows of the room facing them were pockmarked with broken panes.

"Not exactly the place for a honeymoon," Grimaldi said, his low whisper coming in clear as a bell through Bolan's earpiece.

"You got that right," Bolan replied, as much to test the radios as anything else.

They came to a break in the high shrubbery and bushes, and Bolan gestured for Grimaldi to go to the right. He hated separating this early, but knew they didn't have the time to stay together for a perimeter search. At least the limited range of the radios allowed them to communicate with each other while out of sight.

Bolan circled to his left constantly scanning the area. The

shrubbery gave way to a semiclear area at the back of the building that had once been paved to form an outdoor terrace of sorts. He noticed more weeds popping up through the hard surface. Spiderwebs suspended from the building to the bushes glowed in the sunlight, and he took this as a good sign that no one had passed through here recently. He glanced at the ground, as well. A fine layer of sandy dust lay undisturbed on the sidewalk. Bolan reached the edge of the building and slowed.

"At the southwest corner now," Bolan said. "Looks all clear so far. Undisturbed terrain."

"Roger that," came Grimaldi's reply. "The front's clear."

The back portion of the hotel was deserted. More dust and spiderwebs convinced Bolan that no one had traversed this area in a while. He brought the Beretta close to his chest and continued walking, checking the windows and rear entrance, all of which were boarded up and showed no signs of having been recently opened.

"Coming around," Grimaldi said in his ear.

"Roger that," Bolan confirmed.

He saw his partner step into view, his SIG-Sauer held at the ready in front of his chest.

"The front's open but hasn't been used," Grimaldi said. "Unless Spider-Man's been here to help out with some fast web-spinning."

"He's too busy making movies," Bolan said. They tagged up and went back around. The soldier surveyed the enormous web structure spanning the archway leading to the front entrance. The spider had been busy indeed.

"Maybe our buddy Lee will be expecting to see this, too," Bolan said. "We'd be better off going in from another angle."

Grimaldi pointed to the large double doors at the end of the entrance walkway. "Not to mention having to slip that damn lock." He looked up at the nearest balcony. Its jutting concrete base was perhaps ten or eleven feet above his head. The banister of the lower room stood at about four feet, which made for a handy step-up to the next level. "Doable for you and me, as long as you don't mind boosting our British friends."

"Okay, I'll boost Danser," Bolan said with a grin. "You can do Fawkes."

He did one more quick check. He still didn't like it, but at this point they were fighting the clock and it was the only game in town. Grimaldi went to get the two Brits while Bolan waited by the entrance. Everything seemed to be undisturbed and going according to Fawkes's plan, but something still gnawed at Bolan. It seemed like everything was falling into place, and he was always suspicious whenever it was too easy. He began replaying the plan in his mind, trying to figure out if he'd overlooked something. Sometimes the smallest detail was right there in front, waiting to be seen.

Or heard, he thought as the faint syncopation of the rotor blades became distinct once more. The helicopter was coming back. The docked boat had been an obvious sign of their presence. He had underestimated Lee's foresight. Or had the whole thing been a setup all along?

Bolan stepped out to see where exactly Grimaldi and the others were and saw them running up the walkway about twenty yards from him.

The rotor noise grew louder, the sound indicating an increase in speed. The pilot was bringing it in faster. Bolan scanned the sky. The helicopter was still a minute, black dragonfly but getting larger by the second. He had to assume that if they couldn't see them already, they knew where to look. The party was about to begin.

Not good, Bolan thought.

He ran forward and vaulted the banister for the patio of one of the first-floor rooms. Grimaldi and the others came running up. Bolan motioned for them to do the same. Fawkes made it over with little trouble, and Grimaldi swept Danser into his arms and set her on the other side.

"Let me help you, ma'am," he said.

"I could have bloody well made it over myself," she said.

"Sorry," Grimaldi told her, "but we're in kind of a hurry here."

Bolan took out his Espada knife and pried off a couple of the low boards covering the patio-style doors and then kicked them open. He set the boards down and told Fawkes and Danser to get inside. The helicopter sounded closer.

Danser hesitated momentarily, getting on her hands and knees. It looked like Grimaldi was about to slap her on the butt when he hesitated.

That was Jack, Bolan thought, allowing himself a quick grin. Always the gentleman.

"Move it," Bolan said. "Go through to the back and into the woods. You should find more cover there, and go to escape and evasion tactics."

"What about you?" Grimaldi asked, glancing at the approaching Puma.

"I'll see if I can slow them down a bit and meet you in the woods."

Fawkes scrambled through next and then Grimaldi. Bolan remained on the outside and quickly grabbed the boards and shoved them back into place. With a few hard kicks he'd secured them enough to obscure the tampering. He refolded the knife and clipped it back inside his pants as he glanced up at the sky again. The helicopter slowed as it approached the expanse of sandy beach.

Bolan jumped on the banister, reached up and grabbed the floor of the balcony directly above him. Once his fingers had purchase, he began pulling himself upward, lacing his fingers through the decorative concrete tiles like he was scaling a climbing wall. As he was suspended about fifteen feet above the ground, one of the decorative flourishes snapped loose and he almost lost his grip, hanging by one arm. The rotor blades continued to slow and Bolan immediately resumed his climb, reaching the banister and pulling himself up and over. He rolled across the balcony, checking the helicopter's progress as he kicked at some of the low boards covering this patio doorway entrance. The boards split in two, leaving a foot-high crawl space.

The Puma's rotors slowed to a stop and Bolan saw the side doors slide open. He watched and counted as seven men disembarked from the right side, six from the left, all carrying rifles and submachine guns. Sixteen plus a crew of three… That left three more possible wildcards if Grimaldi had been right on the money. From the looks of it, these guys meant business.

Bolan watched as the new arrivals crossed the sandy beach and headed toward the high concrete wall. The group moved at a fair speed and with a modicum of tactics, each man periodically flattening on the ground after about twenty yards with his rifle aimed toward the hotel to allow the next man to move forward.

The group didn't look like run-of-the-mill Triad hoods, either. They wore the olive-drab uniforms of Chinese army regulars. A couple had Type 56 rifles, the Chinese version of the old Kalashnikov AK-47 standby, with banana-clip magazines. That meant thirty 7.62 mm rounds coming at him at almost two thousand feet per second. The rest had Type 85 submachine guns and a variety of pistols. He noticed one guy with a handgun was a tall Caucasian in a black jumpsuit with blue stripes up the side. He was the one calling the shots. Bolan recognized him.

Simmons.

Two of the men branched off and headed for the yacht. This was definitely a planned operation and not some random discovery on a routine scouting mission. They had been set up, all right.

Bolan flattened out on the floor of the balcony and flipped down the foregrip on his Beretta 93-R. The weapon had a selector lever for 3-round bursts, but he kept it at single shots for the moment. The foregrip gave him better stability for any long-range shots but Bolan knew better than to waste what precious ammunition he had as his adversaries moved up the beach. The time to hit them would be right as they began scaling the wall. If he could pin them down there, it would buy the others some time.

A burst of gunfire echoed from somewhere inside the building behind him.

Bolan pressed the transmit button on his throat mike. "Sitrep."

"The party's started," Grimaldi said. "They must have dropped off another contingent earlier that was working its way around to the back."

"How many?"

Bolan heard Grimaldi swear, then the echo of more gunshots. "Can't tell right now. At least a couple."

"I got about a dozen working their way up to the front, too," Bolan said. "I'll be engaging shortly."

"Roger that."

Bolan watched the first men dip out of sight as they got to the wall. They'd probably be forming a human pyramid and then pull the others up by ropes once they had one or two up top. It was a standard wall-ascending tactic. If these guys were Chinese army regulars, it was safe to assume they'd be trained in military procedures. And if Simmons was former MI-6, he'd probably have a good grasp of assault tactics, too. Bolan's mind flashed to Danser and Fawkes and he wondered how effective they'd be in this fight.

Had they ever been under fire?

Fawkes mentioned he'd been in the Royal Navy, so hopefully he had some fight in him. Danser seemed young and inexperienced, but Bolan hoped she would rise to the occasion.

He did a quick ammo assessment. He had a full load plus one in the chamber of his Beretta, and four more 20-round magazines. That made his total 101. Grimaldi's SIG-Sauer P-226 had a 15-round magazine capacity plus the option of keeping one in the pipe. Adding two additional magazines plus his little .38 snubby and his total was fifty-three. Assuming both Danser and Fawkes had the standard Walther PPKs with eight rounds each, that would be sixteen more. He didn't remember seeing any spare magazines on either of them. Bolan allowed himself a grim smile. They were on a low-ammo alert before the party even got started.

The first three men slid up over the wall, one assuming a cover position with a Type 85 submachine gun. The other two men stood on the wall and dropped ropes down, then began pulling back as the men below ran up the wall using the extended ropes.

It's time, Bolan thought, and centered the Beretta's sights on the sentry. He squeezed off a round, catching the man in the chest, and was already acquiring target acquisition on the new guy coming up the wall to the right.

The sound suppressor on the Beretta reduced the explosion of the weapon to a discreet cough. The man's head exploded as he came up over the wall. Bolan adjusted his aim again, picking off the man holding the rope, peripherally seeing him tumble down toward the beach. The Executioner hit the second rope man squarely in the back, figuring the guy ascending this one's rope was too obscure.

Low-ammo alert, he reminded himself. Have to make every shot count.

Four down, probably fifteen to go, including the crew. A couple of rifle barrels edged over the top of the concrete wall and started spitting fire.

"Sounds like you've joined the party," Grimaldi said over the earpiece.

Bolan didn't answer, not wanting to reach down to activate the throat mike. He moved back as a flurry of rounds perforated the horizontally nailed boards covering the patio door behind him. They had to have pinpointed his position already. Maybe somebody in the helicopter had binoculars.

He hoped it wasn't a thermal image scanner. That would be real trouble even if they made it to the woods. More rounds skittered over the concrete slab of the balcony. They were firing upward and their rounds were going high, but it was most likely only covering fire designed to buy time. Simmons probably had some of his men advancing from the side, plus there was still the gunners to contend with at the back door.

More rounds zipped into the balcony, smacking into the wooden boards and chipping away at the ceramic ornamentations of the balcony screen.

Can't go down, Bolan thought. No choice but to go back. He rolled toward the fractured boards and squirmed inside. The room was dark and full of cobwebs. The sticky tendrils clung to his face as he brushed through them. The room was empty of any furnishings. He could make out a bathroom sink and a toilet off to the left, the door standing open. The cracks between the boards allowed slats of sunlight through, and Bolan made his way to the door leading to the hallway of the second floor. He opened it cautiously. After taking a quick look in each direction, Bolan headed for the staircase, which was on the opposite wall. It faced the main entrance and once they got over the outside wall that was the way they'd most likely come in.

He rounded the last corner and keyed his mike.

"Sitrep," he said.

A burst of gunfire was his immediate reply, then Grimaldi's voice. "Holding on, but the Brits are almost out of ammo."

"They're breaching the front door," Bolan said as he saw the double doors buckle. He lined up his body behind a solid stone pillar, exposing as little of himself as possible. "I'm still on the second floor. If you can move into the main lobby, we can catch them in a cross fire."

"On my way."

Bolan watched the front doors fly outward and two men entered. One was holding a crowbar, which he dropped as he took up his slung rifle, and the other a submachine gun. They moved cautiously through the small foyer, each pausing and flattening against the wall below the bricked archway. More men entered, holding their rifles and machine guns in the ready position. The first two maintained their positions against the wall as the second group advanced.

"I'm ready whenever you are," Grimaldi's voice whispered in Bolan's ear.

Bolan knew the Stony Man pilot would wait for him to fire first, and he wanted to let a few more of them get into the kill zone. Simmons came behind the group in the foyer and swore.

"Go on, get in there," his harsh voice said. "Are you afraid of three men and a woman?"

More of the soldiers moved inside, and Bolan used his thumb to flip his selector switch to 3-round-burst mode. Just as Simmons moved to the front and began to give more orders, Bolan put a burst in each of the two soldiers closest to the archway. Grimaldi's fire came next, taking out the ones who'd managed to advance the farthest. Simmons swore again and immediately dropped to the floor, scrambling back toward the broken front doors.

Four more down, eleven to go, Bolan thought.

"Help yourself to their guns," Bolan said as he concentrated another burst toward the front doors. "I'll cover you."

"Thanks a lot," Grimaldi said.

Bolan fired again as the door edged open. Below him Grimaldi dashed forward and grabbed a rifle and submachine gun, then ran back.

Bolan emptied his magazine at the doorway, dropped it as the slide locked back and withdrew one of the magazines from his belt holster that contained the armor-piercing rounds. He slammed the magazine home just as a new group stormed through the opening, their guns firing wildly.

Bolan ducked behind the cover of the pillar, then rotated to the other side. He'd been on the left side of it originally, and most of the hostile rounds were pulling to that side. He brought the Beretta up and fired off two 3-round bursts at the new intruders. Three of them tumbled forward. No sign of Simmons.

"Jack," Bolan said as he left his cover position and sprinted down the hallway. "I'm going to hit their flank."

"Roger that. Watch it."

Bolan kept running straight toward the doorway of the room on the corner. He planted a kick under the doorknob, and the door flew backward. This room was darker than the one on the other side had been, but it was also empty. Bolan moved straight through, mentally calculating how many adversaries they had left.

Assuming there were eight more, including the crew and Simmons, and at least two of them were involved in the rear attack, that meant he had at least six more to take out. He got to the flimsy, wooden patio doors that led to the balcony, ripped them open and then slammed his shoulder against the securing horizontal boards. He crouched and scanned the area through the arabesque design of the balcony screen. Below he saw Simmons, half-concealed by the corner, directing four soldiers to go inside the patio doors of a first-floor room.

Bolan rose enough to extend his Beretta over the banister and took out all four of the soldiers with three bursts of fire. Simmons glanced upward, his face a mixture of shock and confusion. Bolan squeezed off another 3-round burst that sent a cloud of broken concrete chips flying in the air around the Englishman's head. He whirled back, grabbing his shoulder.

Bolan switched out magazines, vaulted over the banister and dropped the sixteen feet to the ground, his leg muscles absorbing the shock with a punishing jolt. He kept moving, peppering each of the four fallen soldiers with a precautionary burst as he advanced, picking up one of their rifles as he ran. It was a QZB-03 model—a light assault weapon with full- and semi-auto capabilities. Effective range was about 400 meters, just about right for what he had in mind.

"I'm going to take out the group in the Puma," Bolan said, keying his mike with his thumb. He wasn't sure if his voice would be distinct on the run. "They already sent two men to the boat."

"Roger that," came Grimaldi's reply. "This Type 56, Kalashnikov rip-off did the trick so far. No hostile fire coming from the rear."

"Move up to the front and help me then," Bolan said. He rounded the corner and saw the blood trail. Twenty yards ahead Simmons dropped and rolled over the concrete wall leading to the beach. "That bird's our best ticket out of here."

Bolan slowed and watched as the Englishman regained his shaky footing and began running toward the helicopter. The rotors began a slow, startup rotation and the soldier dropped to the ground as he got to the edge of the walkway, placing the barrel of the rifle on the beveled edge of the tide wall. He adjusted the rear sight as peripherally he tracked Simmons's progress toward the idling chopper.

He had about fifty yards to go.

The Englishman fell, then got to his feet, waving his arms.

Bolan placed his cheek against the stock and keyed his mike.

"Move on up and cover my six," he said.

"Roger that," Grimaldi said. "On the way."

Bolan was distracted by the worry that they hadn't taken out all the hostiles, but he knew he couldn't let Simmons get to the chopper and take off. That would change their escape into a delayed turkey shoot, when more reinforcements got under way from Lee. No, this had to end here and now.

He closed his left eye and sighted along the barrel, centering on Simmons. The Englishman's movement slowed from a jog to a walk and then a stumbling gait.

The side door of the helicopter popped open. Two men got

out and ran toward Simmons. Bolan adjusted his sight picture to the farthest one, giving him lead time to get to Simmons, then centered on the Puma's front windshield. The AS 332 was still on the ground. Better to keep it there than to risk it taking off and crashing.

The helicopter rose a few feet, canted to the left and settled back on the sand. The sun beat directly onto the windshield, obscuring the view inside. Bolan waited, trying to approximate where the pilot would be on the other side of the Plexiglas shield. The other two crew members had reached Simmons. They lifted him by his arms and began a quick trot back toward the Puma.

The sun turned the windshield into a shimmering mirror of gold.

The two crew members were half dragging Simmons now, about twenty feet from the helicopter.

The pilot rotated the AS 332 slightly, rising only a foot or so upward before settling back, changing the angle so the open door would allow the three men easy access.

Bolan lined up the sights in that fleeting instant and squeezed the trigger. The piercing scream of the round going off instantly cut off his hearing, giving way to a humming deafness. The pilot jerked and slumped forward. The rotors of the Puma bobbled uneasily for a few seconds and slowed to a stop. Bolan adjusted the sight picture to the crewman holding Simmons's left arm.

Crack!

The crewman arched backward for a moment then whipped forward toward the sand. The second crewman dropped Simmons, who slumped to his knees. Bolan sighted in on the running man, giving him a slight lead, and squeezed off another round. The crewman fell in midstride.

Bolan felt a tap on his leg and looked around.

Grimaldi grinned back at him and mouthed, "Nice shooting."

Bolan realized his hearing was still inactive. He got up and saw Fawkes and Danser bringing up the rear. She looked as white as a ghost, and her face was a frozen mask of fear. Fawkes looked grim but determined. Bolan glanced around and motioned them toward the wall.

"Watch me and do what I do," he said to them. To him, his voice sounded like it was funneled through a long tunnel. Grimaldi turned and held his rifle at the ready position, watching their backs as Bolan knelt on the edge of the wall, hooking his left hand and left foot on the edge of the concrete lip at the top. He held the rifle in his right hand and flattened against the wall, extending himself downward while still holding on at the top. When his body was completely flattened against the surface of the wall, he quickly unhooked his left foot and then his hand as his legs descended. He dropped to the sand a second later.

Danser and Fawkes looked at each other. Fawkes motioned for her to go first. She got into position but started to slip. Fawkes grabbed her arm and Bolan got her legs, lifting her down to the sand. Fawkes went next, followed by Grimaldi who executed the spider-crawl movement with accomplished ease.

Bolan motioned them to head toward the helicopter and waited as they passed him, his gaze shifting from the top of the wall to the boat, looking for more hostiles. There was no way he was certain all of the enemy had been effectively neutralized. Simmons bothered him, too, but he knew Grimaldi would check him. A bullet would have been safer, but Bolan thought the Englishman might have some intelligence value. He did a quick glance over his shoulder at their progress. They were perhaps twenty yards from the Puma now. Bolan began a steady backward run, made awkward by the unevenness of the sandy beach.

"I'll cover your six," Grimaldi's voice said in Bolan's ear

among a humming noise that told him his hearing was gradually returning to normal. "You can quit all that backstepping."

"Check out Simmons," Bolan said, keying his own mike as he turned and began a quickening trot toward the chopper. What he saw next unfolded in a series of slow-motion movements, like the flickering of an old-time silent movie.

Grimaldi was pointing and yelling while keeping his rifle trained in the direction of the old hotel.

Fawkes moved toward the still-prone Simmons.

Danser was on the other side of the helicopter pulling the pilot out from behind the controls.

Suddenly, Simmons made a jerking movement, turning and getting to his knees while extending his right arm, which recoiled. He was holding a pistol.

Bolan heard a distant popping sound.

Fawkes curled forward, holding his chest.

Bolan slowed as he was bringing his rifle up to acquire a sight picture on Simmons, but Grimaldi made a quick sidestepping movement and slashed downward at Simmons's arm with the rifle. The Englishman dropped his weapon and Grimaldi followed up with a rifle butt-strike to the man's face.

Simmons flipped backward as if he'd been poleaxed.

Bolan quickened his pace and was there in about thirty-five more seconds. Grimaldi was holding the end of the rifle barrel against the back of Simmons's head. The Englishman's face was jammed into the sand, particles flying in a little cloud in front of his mouth with each ragged breath.

"Go ahead and move, you son of a bitch," Grimaldi said. "Give me an excuse."

Danser ran around the front of the Puma and screamed in frustration, "Oh, my God, Hugh. No."

Bolan surveyed the scene behind them. Still no sign of hostiles, but that didn't mean anything. He slung the rifle and picked up Fawkes under the arms, dragging him through the sand toward the helicopter. He opened the door and yelled for Danser to get in first. She did and helped him lift Fawkes onto the floor area. Bolan spied a pair of plastic handcuffs stashed in the seat flap and grabbed them. He jumped back and ran to Simmons, roughly grabbing the man's arms and twisting them behind his back.

Simmons grunted and swore. "I'm wounded, for God's sake."

"Shut up," Grimaldi said, giving the man's head a poke with the rifle barrel.

Bolan pulled the plastic cuffs tight, securing Simmons's hands. He glanced back at the hotel, then up at Grimaldi.

"Let's get out of here."

Grimaldi lifted the Puma off the beach like he was pulling out of a spot in an empty parking lot. He banked the craft to the right and headed out over the water.

"Where to now?" he yelled.

Bolan considered the situation for a brief second and shouted to Danser. "Is there a helipad on the roof of the British Embassy?"

Distracted, she asked him to repeat the question.

He did and she nodded.

"Good," Bolan said. "That's where we're going. Use your cell phone to call them and tell them to have a trauma team waiting for us." He pointed down at Fawkes, who lay on the hard metal floor, the blood leaking from his right side.

Danser took out her cell phone, dialed and held the device to one ear, covering the other with her free hand.

Simmons lay on his side, still trussed up with the plastic handcuffs keeping his arms secured behind his back, about four feet from the door. The right shoulder of his blue jumpsuit was dark with blood. Danser was across from him, giving the man an evil stare as she spoke into the phone. Bolan took out his folding knife and cut away the front of Fawkes's jacket and shirt. Both were soaked with blood and Bolan noticed a frothy, pulsating wound sight in the man's midchest. No exit wound. Fawkes was semiconscious, and Bolan leaned close to him and spoke loudly in his ear to be heard over the vibrating helicopter engine.

"You're going to be all right," Bolan told him. He actually didn't know if Fawkes would survive, given the amount of blood he was losing and the apparent sucking chest wound. He scanned the cabin for something to dress the wound. The inside of the Puma was virtually devoid of anything that he could use.

Danser flipped her phone closed and shouted to Bolan, "They're expecting us."

He motioned to her. "See if you can find a first-aid kit, or something thin, plastic and flexible that I can use to cover this," he said, pointing at the crimson bubbles forming and bursting on Fawkes's chest. He gathered the torn shirt and used that as a temporary compress. Danser sprang into action, opening every compartment in the cabin. As she pulled at the back of a pouch on the back of the pilot's seat, a plastic-coated page fell out. She looked down, grabbed it and handed it to Bolan.

He grinned. "This might do the trick. Ready to play Florence Nightingale?"

"I beg your pardon?"

"Never mind." He took the plastic page and told her to take over holding the compress. When her small hands had replaced his, Bolan used his knife to slice the plastic-coated page into four roughly equal-size sections, each about four inches in diameter and length. He refolded the knife and clipped it onto his belt. He then gently pulled Danser's hands away, removed the cloth compress and placed one of the plastic sections over the wound, collapsing the bubbles that had accumulated there. She looked at him.

"Sucking chest wound," he yelled back. "We've got to keep it sealed or his lung will collapse."

Danser nodded.

Bolan pressed the plastic against the wound to try to stem

the bleeding, then grabbed one of Danser's hands and placed it over the site.

"Keep applying firm pressure here," he said. "If his chest starts to swell, raise one of the corners a little bit to release the pressure. Got it?"

She nodded, then her eyes showed a flash of panic. "Where are you going?"

"To talk to him." Bolan grinned as he cocked his head toward Simmons. He made sure the grin wasn't a nice one. Simmons was watching them.

Bolan took out the knife and flipped the blade open in front of the supine Englishman's face. He held it there momentarily, then grabbed the blood-soaked material of the jumpsuit and sliced it open. After inspecting the wound, he folded the knife and clipped it to his belt again.

"How bad does it look?" Simmons asked.

Bolan ignored him.

"I asked how badly am I hurt, you bloody bastard," Simmons shouted.

Bolan was about to reply when Danser beat him to it.

"You're the bloody bastard," she shouted, her mouth twisting with hatred. "You're a traitor and you shot poor Hugh."

Simmons looked away and shook his head. Bolan grabbed the man's jaw and twisted his head back so the two were face-to-face. The Executioner leaned forward.

"How did Eddie Lee know we'd be on the island?" he asked.

"Go screw yourself," Simmons said through clenched teeth.

"Were those Chinese regular troops?" Bolan asked.

Simmons puckered his lips and tried to spit. Bolan twisted the man's mouth to the side.

"Try that again, asshole," he said, "and I'll show you how much I already don't like you."

"Toss that piece of crap out the door," Grimaldi yelled

from the pilot's seat. "We can see how many points he gets for the dive."

"You wouldn't dare," Simmons said.

Bolan shoved the man's head away and reached over with his left hand to grab the door handle, turning it downward and sliding the side door partially open. The wind whistled through the cabin with jolting force and the helicopter bucked and swayed. Grimaldi made some adjustment on the stick and the AS 332's forward motion smoothed out a bit.

"Go ahead," Grimaldi yelled. "Throw out the trash."

Bolan picked up the two Chinese rifles, removed the magazines and popped the rounds from the chambers. He set them on the floor next to Simmons's face and leaned down again.

"I'm going to ask you some questions now," Bolan said. "And for every nonresponse, or smart-ass answer, something's going out the door. Get it?" He picked up the magazines and waited. When Simmons said nothing, Bolan tossed the magazine into the blue expanse beyond the open door. He picked up the Type 56 rifle.

"How did Lee know we'd be at the hotel?"

Simmons pursed his lips again, remaining silent.

Bolan shrugged and tossed the rifle out the door. He then picked up the QZB-03 rifle.

"Were those Chinese regulars who were with you?" he asked.

Simmons licked his lips.

Bolan tossed the rifle through the door.

"Now," he said, "we're getting down to the wire here." He stepped over Simmons, flipped him onto his stomach and grabbed the man by the back of his neck and pants.

"Who are Eddie Lee's new clients?" Bolan yelled.

Simmons's mouth opened and closed, but he said nothing.

"Toss out the trash," Grimaldi yelled. "He's stinking up the place."

Bolan moved toward the door, carrying Simmons across the space. He paused at the door.

"Wait! Stop!" Simmons yelled. "You can't do this."

"Yeah, I can," Bolan said.

"How long can you tread water?" Grimaldi yelled.

"Tread water?" Bolan said with a sly grin. "Hell, the fall will probably kill him."

"Let me get down lower then." The smile on Grimaldi's face was positively malevolent. The Puma slowed and began to dip downward. "I'll hover a bit and we can watch the sharks having some fun."

The Executioner moved a step closer to the open door, holding Simmons so his head was outside.

"No," Simmons screamed. "Pull me back in, pull me back in."

Bolan did so.

"He didn't say please," Grimaldi said.

Bolan knew that the pilot was just playing along because he knew the Executioner, who was also known as Sergeant Mercy in the old days, would not have tossed the traitorous Englishman out the door. The threat alone, as Bolan figured, had been enough to break the man.

Bolan roughly slammed Simmons back down on the floor, moving his face directly in front of the other's man's ear.

"One more chance," Bolan shouted. "And keep in mind that I don't play games. How did Lee know when we were on the island?"

"We were tipped on that," Simmons said sullenly.

"By who?"

Simmons shook his head. "I don't know. He wouldn't tell me."

"Wrong answer." Bolan got up and grabbed the man by the collar again and headed for the still-open door.

"All right, all right, I'll tell you," Simmons said. "It was Cleeves."

Bolan glanced over toward Danser, whose eyes widened.

"Why would Cleeves tip him off?" Bolan asked.

The air seemed to be draining out of Simmons. His head drooped until his chin rested on his chest.

Bolan shook him. "Why?"

Simmons raised his head slightly. "He's been in Lee's pocket for a long time. He's got a bit of a gambling problem."

"Who were those Chinese that were with you today?"

Simmons took a few quick breaths, as though he was trying to recover from a quick sprint. "You had that one right. Chinese army regulars. Lee's uncle loaned them to us."

"Who are the new clients?"

"That, I don't know," Simmons said. "You've got to believe me."

"My bullshit meter's already at full," Bolan said, tugging the man's collar again. "Who are they?"

"Arabs," Simmons said quickly. "Arabs from some Middle Eastern country. One's named Shahkhia. Some dictator's son, or something to that effect. That's all I know. Please. Believe me."

Bolan adjusted his grip on the man's collar, rolling the material of the jumpsuit in his fist to tighten it around the man's neck. "What does 'Sleeping Dragons' mean?"

"It's…" Simmons hesitated and Bolan made another half roll with his fist. Simmons's face reddened. "It's some kind of Chinese army superweapon. His uncle has access to it. That's all I know. Please."

Bolan glanced toward Grimaldi, who shrugged. "We're a couple of minutes out. I could use Danser up here to talk me in."

Bolan released Simmons, letting his spent form fall to the metal floor. He stepped over and slammed the side door shut then knelt beside Danser, gently replacing her hand with his. The wound needed to be depressurized anyway. He peeled back a corner of the plastic and let some air escape.

"Go up front and help Jack guide this bird home," he said to her.

Her face looked drawn and wan. "On one condition."

Bolan cocked his head inquisitively.

Danser managed a weak smile. "That you continue to play the lady with the lamp until we get settled."

Bolan grinned. "You got a deal."

Winston Cleeves sat in his apartment fingering the latest folded paper dragon that he'd found outside his door with his newspaper and listening to Cheshire Regiment's rousing version of "Steadfast and True." It was late afternoon…very late, and Cleeves hadn't heard anything concerning the Imperial Palace fiasco. At least he assumed it had been a fiasco for the two Yanks. Danser and Fawkes would be collateral damage, so to speak, but all things considered, that was unavoidable. At any rate, the dragon was a sign that Lee wanted to speak with him again.

Cleeves picked up one of the disposable cell phones and dialed the familiar number. Hopefully it would be an update that everything had gone as planned and he'd have to make calls to his superiors and the Americans about the unfortunate turn of events.

Lee answered with an uncharacteristic gruffness, and Cleeves immediately took it to mean that perhaps something unforeseen had occurred.

"Whatever is wrong?" he asked.

"Things did not go as planned," Lee said. "The Americans got away and wiped out a squad of men."

"Good heavens. What on earth happened?"

"Who are these Americans? You did not tell me they were so formidable."

Cleeves took a deep breath. "What about my two operatives? Any word on them?"

"I don't know. After hearing nothing I sent another group to search. They found almost the entire squad of PLA regulars butchered. The helicopter and Simmons were missing. The boat your man rented was still at the dock on the island."

Cleeves considered that. Apparently calling the Americans merely "formidable" was a bit of an understatement. "PLA regulars? How many did you send?"

"Fifteen, plus Simmons and my helicopter crew. Almost all dead. Now my uncle is upset at having to arrange a 'training accident' to account for the missing soldiers." Lee exhaled sharply. "I hold you responsible for this."

Cleeves licked his lips, wondering exactly how this scenario had played out. The fact that Simmons was not found among the dead was a bit troubling. Could he have been taken prisoner?

And if so, Cleeves thought, how much does he know about me?

"Now see here," he said, trying to regain the initiative. "Blaming me because *your* men couldn't take care of two Yanks is a bit of a stretch, don't you think?"

"I think you are quickly proving to be more of a liability than an asset," Lee said. His tone was terse, demanding. "Find out about Simmons, and what the Americans know, and call me back. I am in the middle of an important negotiation and cannot risk premature exposure."

From what Cleeves had secretly gathered himself, he knew more than he let on about this "important negotiation." He recited what he hoped sounded like a positive bit of reassurance, but when no reply came he realized Lee had already terminated the call. He closed the cell phone and set it on the desk. It was time for a reassessment. If things had gone as badly as Lee said, the Yanks were bound to be suspicious that the whole thing was a setup. He let the ramifications of the unfolding situation drift away as the as Cheshire Regiment now began to play "A Bridge Too Far."

Prophetic? He wondered how this was all going to conclude, and how long he'd have to wait.

Since I was the primary architect, he thought, this isn't shaping up the way I intended. A shadow from the fading afternoon sunlight crossed his desk and the music finally stopped.

He heard the outer door of his office open and then saw the big American, Cooper, heading toward him holding a pistol with an ominous-looking sound suppressor. Right behind him were Danser and the other American.

No, he thought, this wasn't what I'd intended at all.

BOLAN TOLD THEM to turn the music up louder as he stepped into the adjacent room and called Stony Man Farm on his sat phone. He punched in the number and played with the folded paper dragon he'd taken from Cleeves's desk as the phone rang. Brognola answered sounding tired and cranky.

"Rise and shine, sunshine," Bolan said. "It's got to be what, 6:00 a.m.?"

"It's 6:35," Brognola said, "and I haven't gone to bed yet."

"Welcome to my world. You get anything useful on Winston Cleeves?"

"What the hell is that in the background?"

"Marching music," Bolan said. "Thought you might need some inspiration."

"Yeah, right. Aaron's been tracing Cleeves's finances as well as those of Eddie Lee. Found a few interesting wrinkles. One of Lee's dummy companies has supposedly been shipping 'medical supplies' out of Hong Kong to Libya by way of Egypt. Lee's also got quite a bankroll in the Cayman Islands. As far as Cleeves goes, we're working on a tentative lead on him with a bank in Switzerland."

"I'm getting ready to interrogate him now."

"What?"

"He set us up. He's got to be dirty. We grabbed him at his place, but MI-6 has got to be on the way."

"Maybe it'd be better to let them talk to him. After all, it is their agency's mess to clean up."

"We don't have time to wait," Bolan said. "We're still trying to get a handle on this Sleeping Dragons thing. Plus, I'm assuming Cleeves never sent you those surveillance photos of Eddie Lee's Middle Eastern clients to run through facial recognition, right?"

"Hell, no." Brognola snorted. "Middle Eastern. Damn, I'm not liking the sound of this."

"Well, you'll like this even less. One of them is supposedly some dictator's son named Shahkhia, and he's here to buy the Sleeping Dragons."

"You figure out what that might be yet?" Brognola asked.

"Not a clue other than it's some kind of superweapon."

"Shahkhia…" Brognola's heavy breathing was audible. "Shahkhia… You know, there's a rumor that Khadaffi had an illegitimate son named Mustapha. What the hell was his full name?"

"You're asking me?" Bolan said.

"No, smart-ass, I was being rhetorical." Bolan heard him working the end of a cigar. "Mustapha Ahmad Shahkhia. That's it."

"Shahkhia? That has a familiar sound to it."

"It should," Brognola said. "I think you and Jack tangled with someone named Shahkhia a while back in that country, didn't you?"

Bolan blew out a slow breath. "That's like asking Celise Boyer how many guys she's kissed."

"Celise Boyer? What the hell are you talking about now?"

"Forget it. I've been hanging with Grimaldi too long." He glanced at his watch, figuring they had perhaps less than an hour before the MI-6 contingent arrived and took custody of Cleeves. "I have to go. Time to do the good cop, bad cop routine."

"Let me guess who's going to be the bad cop," Brognola said. "See what you can find out and call me back ASAP. I'll be waiting."

"Have Aaron fix you a cup of his special coffee," Bolan said.

"Hell," Brognola said with a laugh, "I'm not that desperate."

Bolan said goodbye to Brognola and let the folded paper dragon flutter to the floor.

LEE WATCHED THROUGH the crack in the door as Mustapha Shahkhia and his bodyguard both leaned forward on the small rugs, touching their foreheads to the floor, their arms stretched out in front of them, praying. He was tired of dealing with their constant peculiarities and religious quirks. If this was to be his final deal, it was imperative to get moving. Plus, he still had his dear uncle to deal with and anticipated more quirks at that juncture. He wanted the transactions completed by the end of business this day, and the final payment in his account. The city of his birth was suddenly becoming hot. Very hot.

Lee watched and listened to the cadence of their whispered words. He understood none of it, except that it made them ultimately more predictable. Shahkhia had insisted on Lee finding them a vacant room for afternoon prayer, before he would even consider transferring the money. Lee glanced at his watch and estimated that Uncle Yu had to be en route with the second half of the Sleeping Dragons. It was like arranging the pieces one by one on the *weiqi* board, making preparations for the final offensive. If you moved too soon, your opponent would be tipped off and make a countermove that would throw your strategy off. That's why time was of the essence. Afternoon prayers... Let them pray when this was done. He still had the Americans to deal with.

But that did amuse Lee a bit, more so than the praying. The Americans, especially the big one called Cooper, had proved tougher than Lee had assumed, which was why he now needed Cleeves to set one more trap. And this time he would definitely have to send Wang Sze.

The door opened and Shahkhia and the giant came out, rolling their rugs and placing them in a large duffel bag. The Arab smiled at Lee.

"Ah, thank you for your assistance," he said.

Lee was still feeling miffed. "You may thank me by accelerating the money transfer. I believe we had made that agreement."

The Libyan nodded as he removed his laptop from the carrying case. "It will be done."

Lee waited as Shahkhia sat and opened his laptop and began typing on the keyboard. The Libyan paused after a few moments and looked at Lee with a serious expression.

"As you know," he said, "I had hoped to be on my way back to liberate my country by this time with all that I have purchased. Now, I am beginning to have some troubling reservations."

Lee felt his mouth going dry. Was this buffoon thinking of backing out at this late date?

"This has been an enormous undertaking," Lee said. "Not only are the drones and the first part of the Sleeping Dragons already on the way, but I have also seen to it that the technicians capable of programming the drones and reconfiguring the Sleeping Dragons will accompany you to Libya, as well. What more do you want as a display of my good faith?"

Shahkhia smiled, his white teeth looking stark in contrast to his dark skin and beard. "Giving me both parts of the Sleeping Dragons now would be such a display. Each part, as you took such pains to explain to me, is inert until combined, no?"

"At which time the Sleeping Dragons will awaken, and you shall be on your way to liberating your country from the puppets of the West." Lee forced himself to smile. Never let anyone, ally or opponent, see you sweat, he thought. And he'd never considered the Arab an ally—just an opponent in a separate but simultaneous game. Was there a danger in playing too many games at the same time? He had once seen a *weiqi* master dispatch five different foes, all playing on separate boards, all at the same time.

The Libyan's gaze shifted from Lee to the computer. His fingers moved over the keyboard again, then stopped. "So, just for clarification, the rest of the Sleeping Dragons will definitely be here tonight?"

Lee felt his frustration building but kept it under control, as cool as ice in front of the Arab.

"As I told you, my uncle is in Shenzhen now, obtaining the remainder of the shipment. He will be here later tonight for the exchange. The final exchange."

Shahkhia nodded. "And as I mentioned, it is imperative that I leave Hong Kong no later than eight-thirty."

"The flight has already been arranged," Lee said. "You will be cleared by my uncle to take off from the old military airstrip on the far island. No one will question his orders." He watched as the Libyan pressed a few more keys and then nodded.

"There," he said. "It has been done."

Lee smiled and typed in the account status on his own laptop, waiting for verification before proceeding with further conversation. It was another lesson from the old *weiqi* master: Never move in haste, never trust your opponent's word, and always verify his assurances.

Bolan stood on the other side of the door listening. The interrogation was proceeding at a snail's pace, and he was feeling the time constraint. Not only were they under the gun as far as nailing down this Sleeping Dragons thing, but a new team of MI-6 operatives was en route to take over the "Cleeves matter." By her own estimate Danser wouldn't be in charge more than a few more hours, and even with Fawkes down for the count, it was only her and one other operative, Higgins, whom they had shadowing Eddie Lee. They had to break Cleeves quickly, here and now, or run the risk of missing Lee's transaction. And now that Bolan suspected Mustapha Shahkhia was involved, that wasn't an option.

"Winston, Winston, Winston," Grimaldi was saying, "we need to come to a quick understanding here, pal. A real quick one. Otherwise Jillian and I are going out for a couple of egg rolls and leave you here alone with my partner."

"And how is the redoubtable Mr. Cooper?" Cleeves asked. His tone was robust, friendly, not worried at all.

"You'd better hope you don't have to find out," Grimaldi said. "He's not nearly as easy as I am to talk to."

"A preposition at the end of a sentence," Cleeves said. "My, but you Yanks have no respect for the queen's English."

"We're growing tired of your games, Cleeves," Danser said. "Either start talking or he and I are leaving."

Cleeves answered with a forced laugh. "You and I both

know you wouldn't dare turn me over to that barbarian. A smart man always hedges his bets. Need I remind you of proper Service protocol? Section Five, subsection E, on the humane treatment of those suspected of crimes against the crown." He paused and cleared his throat. "I'll be happy to recite it to you, if you wish, chapter and verse."

"Does it include the part about how you betrayed us to Eddie Lee?" she shot back. "How your actions almost got us all killed and poor Hugh grievously wounded?"

"Tut, tut, my girl," Cleeves said. "Fortunes of war. And do remember to bring me back a spot of tea when you go out for that egg roll."

The sarcastic lilt in his voice was the final straw for Bolan. It was time for the "bad cop" to enter the picture. He pushed open the door and stepped inside. Cleeves was seated in a wooden chair in the middle of the room. His soft, fleshy hands rested on his lap. He looked up and smiled as the soldier entered, but Bolan detected a trace of nervousness around the edges.

"Ah, the redoubtable Mr. Cooper returns," Cleeves said. "Would you care for some crumpets?"

Bolan stared at the man for a solid ten seconds. Cleeves's mouth remained frozen in a half smile. A faint tremor shook his lips.

Bolan reached into his pocket and took out a pair of black leather gloves. He began working his big right hand into one of them, staring at Cleeves the whole time.

"Oh, no, not the gloves," Grimaldi said.

"Time for you two to leave," Bolan said as he worked the glove down over his fingers. He finished, smacked his gloved fist into his palm a few times, testing the resiliency, and then began putting on the left one.

"At least let me put down some paper, or something." Grimaldi turned to Danser. "You have any large sheets of plastic?"

She shook her head.

Grimaldi looked around. “How about some garbage bags? Those will work if we cut a couple of them apart at the seams and spread them out. As long as we have some left to put the bloody ones in when we’re done.”

“I’ll go look,” Danser said, and turned to leave.

“Jillian, where are you going?” Cleeves asked, his voice inadvertently rising a few octaves with incipient panic.

She paused to glance at him, a look of abject disgust on her pretty features. She shook her head and stepped out of the room.

Bolan had finished putting on the left glove and smacked that one into his right palm with a resounding crack. He let a sinister, lips-only smile creep across his mouth. Then he reached down and took out his knife and flipped open the blade with a flick of his wrist. The blade made a snicking sound, followed by a metallic thump as the blade locked.

“I think I’m going to enjoy this,” Bolan said.

“At least wait till she gets back with the garbage bags,” Grimaldi cautioned. “I mean, think about the cleanup.”

“I couldn’t care less about it,” Bolan said. “Now you and Danser get out of here. I’ll call when I’m finished.”

Grimaldi shrugged and made a clucking sound. “You know, Winston, I’m sorry. You didn’t seem like such a bad guy for a Brit.” He raised his eyebrows and cocked a thumb at Bolan. “Oh, did I tell you he’s part Irish?”

Cleeves’s lower lip drooped a bit more. He opened his mouth as if to say something, then stopped and swallowed hard. “See here, do you know what Eddie Lee will do to me if he finds out I betrayed him?”

Grimaldi shrugged again. “Eddie isn’t the one I’d be worried about right now if I were you.”

Danser came in carrying two black, plastic garbage bags. She thrust them out toward Grimaldi. “Will these do?”

"Jillian, please," Cleeves said. His voice sounded brittle now.

Bolan grabbed one of the bags, held it up, then slashed the top and side seams with the knife. He motioned for Danser to place it by Cleeves, who immediately stood.

Bolan stepped forward and delivered a short, but powerful punch to the man's gut. The air whooshed out of Cleeves, and he slumped back down into the chair. Bolan grabbed an empty chair and pulled it in front of the now-seated Cleeves. The soldier grabbed the Englishman's left wrist and raised his arm, spreading Cleeves's hand over the back of the empty chair.

"Want me to tie his hands behind him?" Grimaldi asked, pulling a rubber lamp cord out of the wall socket. "Or a sack over his head?"

"No, I want him to see what's going on," Bolan said. His powerful hand twisted Cleeves's wrist.

"You and Danser can get out now," Bolan said, his voice a low growl. "I don't want her to see this."

Tears rolled down Cleeves's fat cheeks and he began to sob as a sudden and pervasive smell of urine wafted into the air. Danser's eyes widened quickly, then narrowed as she held her nose with one hand and fanned the air with the other. Bolan and Grimaldi exchanged quick glances and the soldier winked.

BOLAN DIDN'T ALLOW Cleeves to change his pants even though the man was talking a mile a minute now. He'd started with the history of him and Eddie Lee, the gambling, the winning streak that soon turned into an incremental, overwhelming debt, the recruitment, and finally the latest bit of treachery involving setting up Bolan and the others.

"I'm cooperating," Cleeves said. "I would be very appreciative if you'd let me change my pants."

"There'll be time for that later," Bolan said, sitting on the edge of the desk and glancing at Grimaldi and Danser who had returned. "Now I want to know about this Sleeping Dragons deal. And keep in mind that I already know a whole lot more than you think I do. So if I catch you in one lie…"

"If that happens," Grimaldi said, "changing your knickers will be the least of your problems."

Cleeves blushed and looked at Danser. Bolan noticed that despite her customary stanch British reserve, she seemed to be fascinated by their interrogation techniques.

"Tell me about Mustapha," Bolan said.

Cleeves bit his lower lip. "Mustapha?"

Bolan frowned and stepped closer. "Mustapha Ahmad Shahkhia. Like I said, we've got a lot more of the pieces than you thought."

Cleeves closed his eyes and shifted in the chair. The movement seemed to make him wince. "Shahkhia is here trying to purchase arms to mount a counteroffensive against the transitional government in Libya."

"No shit, Sherlock," Grimaldi said. "Tell us something we don't know."

"What about Rossi?" Bolan asked. "How did Lee know he was following him?"

Cleeves dipped his eyes downward. "You have to understand, we operate in a very tight intelligence community here. Rossi knew Lee was up to something involving…something serious. He got too close and paid the price."

"Sounds to me like you tipped Lee that Rossi was on to him," Grimaldi said.

Cleeves didn't answer.

Bolan and Grimaldi exchanged glances. The man's silence was as good as an affirmation.

"I have to tell you, Winston," Grimaldi said, "you're not scoring too many points here. You'd better give us something real quick or my friend here is going to think you're trying to run a game on us."

Cleeves looked up at Bolan, who stood over him like a large jungle cat, ready to strike. "What do you want to know?"

"Tell us about Sleeping Dragons," Bolan said.

Cleeves heaved a sigh. "It's a new, superlative nerve gas the Chinese military has secretly developed in violation of the Chinese Weapons Convention. It's a binary gas, inert unless combined, at which time it becomes extremely deadly."

"And that's what Shahkhia's here to buy?" Bolan asked.

Cleeves nodded, then looked down again. "Lee's uncle is a general in the Chinese army. He's able to get practically anything Lee needs."

"What else?" Bolan said, reaching forward and grabbing the man's flabby jowls with his big hand and pulling Cleeves's head upward so their eyes met.

"The delivery system. They managed to steal some of the designs for your Predator drones and reconfigure them to deliver the gas to specific targets. With a handful of them, the Libyan can decimate a large urban area or even play havoc crashing one or two into one of your carriers."

Bolan was already calculating the imminent dangers as the Englishman spoke.

"When's this deal supposed to be finalized?" he asked.

"Tonight," Cleeves said. "The drones and the first part of the gas have already been shipped. Shahkhia's set to leave tonight after he makes the final payment and Lee gives him the second part of the gas."

Bolan's strong fingers pressed into the fleshy jowls. "Where's this happening? And what time?"

"I don't know," Cleeves said. "I just received a paper dragon earlier this afternoon and was supposed to phone Lee back regarding the situation with you."

"You're going to do that now," Bolan said, picking up the prepaid cell phone on the desk and holding it in front of Cleeves's face. "Find out when and where they're meeting."

THE WAGES OF TREACHERY are death, Lee thought as he continued his second phone conversation of the day with Cleeves.

"I say, are you still there?" Cleeves asked.

Lee spoke into the phone as calmly as he could. "Of course. I was just deep in thought."

His only regret was that he would not be the one to deal with the Englishman personally. Lee knew the Brit's own countrymen knew about him now, as well as the Americans. In any case, their attempted ruse hadn't fooled him. Lee would have known by the Englishman's voice that something was wrong, even if he hadn't had his men watching the man's apartment after delivering the paper dragon earlier. The Americans and the female British agent had been interrogating him for more than an hour when this phone call came.

Lee was unimpressed at the Englishman's resolve at not even holding out for an hour, although he had never considered Cleeves to be anything more than a convenient but weak link in the chain. That he had been broken in less than sixty minutes was something Lee had already factored into his overall strategy. And now it was time to turn Cleeves's clumsy betrayal into a tactical advantage. Lee picked up one of the squares of paper he kept on his desk and began making the initial folds.

"So you mentioned that the Americans are getting close?" Lee said. "How close?"

"I'd say quite literally they're breathing down the backs of our necks," Cleeves said.

Lee had no doubt they probably were on the other end of this conversation. It was perhaps the first truthful thing Cleeves had told him that day. "And you have no idea what happened to Simmons?"

"Only that he was reportedly shot," Cleeves said. "I can try to find out more if you wish."

"Yes, that would be good." Lee made two more folds, then paused. "But I need something more from you."

"And what might that be?"

"I need you to keep the Americans occupied tonight," Lee said. "I will be meeting my very special client at Pier 19 at the waterfront."

"On Hong Kong Island?" Cleeves sounded almost breathless.

"Of course. Are you all right?" Lee smiled as he made another fold of the paper.

"Yes, yes, of course. Just feeling a bit of a chill."

"You must watch your health," Lee said. "But can you do this for me? Can you keep the Americans away tonight? It is imperative that I complete this negotiation and exchange."

"Certainly," Cleeves said. "What time shall I…strive for them not to be there?"

Lee almost laughed out loud. He folded the paper two more times. The dragon was almost completed. "Ten-thirty."

"Ten-thirty at Pier 19," Cleeves said. His voice had a relieved tone to it. "I'll make sure they'll be tied up elsewhere. You have my word on that."

"Thank you," Lee said, thinking that the man's word was not worth the weight of this paper dragon. He started to make the final folds, then stopped. No, this one should not be a dragon… Something else perhaps. "I shall make sure you are amply rewarded in the customary fashion."

When Cleeves replied, his words sounded stunted. "That would be appreciated."

"Goodbye, Mr. Cleeves," Lee said. He terminated the call and considered his options. The Americans had been holding Cleeves, obviously forcing him to make the call. Now they'd been given the bait and would no doubt be at Pier 19 waiting to intercept him and Shahkhia…except neither he nor the Arab would be there. A perfect ruse in answer to their deception using Cleeves. But Lee would have to send Wang Sze to do the job this time. That would ensure the Americans troubled him no more.

It was inevitable that the Americans would discover that he'd been instrumental in supplying the Sleeping Dragons to the Arab once he unleashed the gas in Libya. When that happened, Lee's involvement would become known to the Americans and the British, who would in turn confront the Mainland Chinese. The Communists would not be pleased, and Lee already knew how they would react, especially once they discovered his uncle's involvement. Lee knew neither he nor his dear uncle would be left alive. Perhaps it was time for him to leave tonight, as well. Hong Kong was becoming too dangerous for him.

He glanced at the suitcase containing the additional one million in Hong Kong dollars that Yu had demanded, and then at his watch. It was time to meet the general on the island to pick up the rest of the Sleeping Dragons, and then make the final exchange with the Arab.

He adjusted the folds of the paper slightly, changing the dragon into a bird and watched as he mimicked it flapping its wings. The Libyan would not be the only one leaving Hong Kong.

Shahkhia smiled as he read the latest email communication from his ground forces commander in Libya. Not only had they received the first shipment and completed the erection of the antenna, but they had secretly discovered the hotel in which the UN delegation and the American actress were staying. That job had been easy. A television news crew was following the woman every place she went.

A news crew—more propagandists from the West. But that would only give him more hostages to play with. Perhaps he would release a few as a token of his good faith… Or perhaps he would behead a few of the infidels and have it broadcast. The internet and Al Jazeera provided a worldwide format to launch the restoration of his country.

The Libyan stared at the wall, his eyes dreamy, fashioning the scene in his mind: an infidel on his knees, his arms bound behind him, his head pulled back to expose his throat while several hooded members of a death squad holding ceremonial *jambiyas* waited for the command against the background of the green flag.

His fantasy was interrupted as Sultan knocked lightly on the open door.

"Sir, it is time," the giant said. "The helicopter is waiting on the roof."

Shahkhia glared at him for a moment. How dare he interrupt the fantasy? But then reason overtook his passion and he smiled at his most faithful servant.

"In Libya they have already started assembling the drones," he said. "And they will be ready for us at the airfield when we land with the rest of the gas."

Sultan nodded and smiled back. "Soon you will be restored to the greatness you deserve. We will return and continue our jihad."

Their jihad...a holy war... Perhaps he should be addressed as Imam? A holy leader. Shahkhia hadn't thought of himself in that context, but now that he considered it, perhaps it was appropriate. The others looked to him not only for direction, but for spiritual guidance, as well. He was a holy warrior taking back his country, defending his people from the corrupting influences of the West. He would protect his people from the American movie actress—the evil woman who was now in his nation's capital spreading her corruption...exposing her hair and her body with impunity. Once they had her as a captive he would have Sultan shave her head and take away her clothes and place her in the street to be spat upon.

"God is great," he intoned.

It was time to do his final deal with this Chinese disciple of the Asian Satan and move on to fulfill his destiny and realize his greatness.

LEE WATCHED AS the large Chinese military transport helicopter slowly descended and landed about forty yards away from his own Puma. Wang Sze and two of his men stood behind him. The island helipad was deserted, as was the immediate area except for the *Painted Lady* docked nearby. Lee knew that the seven crates containing the second portion of the Sleeping Dragons would fit easily into the Puma. It would not leave any room for transporting many of his men, but that was according to plan.

The military helicopter hung suspended in the air for

several more seconds and then lowered onto the helipad, its whirling rotors slowing with every revolution. The side door opened and two soldiers with submachine guns exited, holding their weapons at the ready. Then his uncle stepped out wearing an olive-drab fatigue uniform and starched cap. The silver star on the crescent of the cap gleamed in the dim lighting reflecting off the dark water. Cho Ming Ho, his uncle's trusted bodyguard, hopped out behind him and started barking orders.

They must know that something untoward is happening, Lee thought. How often do a general and a colonel ride along on a nighttime training exercise carrying part of a binary chemical weapon?

Lee stood his ground and watched as his uncle moved toward him, a sly grin stretched over the older man's face. Yu's eyes darted toward the two items at Lee's feet. One was a long duffel bag and the other was the suitcase containing the money. He turned and yelled to Cho, who shouted for the men to disembark from the helicopter but to stand by.

Lee bowed as his uncle approached and Yu acknowledged it with a quick jerking motion of his head. "Do you have both of the items I requested?"

"It is as you instructed," Lee said. He'd been a bit unsettled at Yu's demand that Lee bring a Type 69-I rocket-propelled grenade launcher in the duffel bag. But he knew the reason why: the general did not want to leave a trail. "I assume you will be leaving the island with me?"

Yu smiled, showing the gold inlays of his teeth. "Correct. And now, there is another matter I wish to have addressed."

Lee figured he knew what this one was, too, but he merely feigned ignorance. "What is that?"

Yu tapped the suitcase with his shiny boot. "I want another one of these."

"That's not possible," Lee said. "I would need time to come up with—"

"Don't play your games with me," Yu said. He turned and snapped his fingers and Cho issued more orders to the soldiers standing in a line by the helicopter. They immediately raised their weapons to their shoulders. Yu turned back to face Lee. "Dear nephew, must we quibble about trifles? You know full well that once I deliver the second part of the Sleeping Dragons to you, my military career will be finished. Do you have any idea what it took to smuggle out this shipment tonight?"

Lee kept his face devoid of emotion. "We had an agreement, dear Uncle."

"And if you want me to betray myself and the People's Liberation Army," Yu said, "you must offer me more than a mere bowl of rice."

Lee said nothing. His uncle's late demand was not something he had failed to anticipate. Still, it was best not to make acquiescence look too easy. "I did offer you more than a bowl of rice."

Yu's mouth turned down at the ends. He turned his head and spit. "It is not enough. And do not insult me by pretending you do not have it."

Lee pretended to be conflicted, then turned and told Wang Sze to get the "second suitcase" from the yacht. The powerful bodyguard nodded and trotted toward the *Painted Lady*. He stopped at the side of the yacht and yelled something to the man on board. The man disappeared momentarily, then returned, flinging a heavily laden duffel bag over the side rail. Wang Sze caught the bag, trotted back to Lee's side and set it on the ground.

Yu's eyes drifted downward, then back to his nephew's face. He cocked an eyebrow.

"One million in U.S. dollars," Lee said. "You may count it if you wish."

Yu stared at him, then shook his head and smiled. He pulled out a QSZ-92 semiautomatic pistol and flipped off the safety. "A total count is not necessary at the moment."

The smiled disappeared, replaced by a more menacing look. "But I do wish to look inside. And make no mistake, if you have betrayed me I will kill you."

"Dear Uncle," Lee said, "have I not anticipated your every wish, your every desire?" He extended his open palm toward the general and then the new duffel bag. "I was planning on presenting that to you once we were on board."

Yu's eyes flashed from his nephew to the duffel bag. "Open it."

Lee waited a moment, then turned to Wang Sze and nodded. The powerful Chinese squatted and pulled open the top zipper. Bundles of U.S. currency were plainly visible.

Yu's eyes lingered on the contents, then returned to Lee. Yu half turned and motioned to Cho who conveyed more instructions to the squad of soldiers. They immediately slung their weapons and began unloading a stack of long wooden crates from the helicopter. One by one they carried the crates to the Puma and loaded them inside. Once they were finished Cho ran up to General Yu and saluted, saying the task was complete.

Yu nodded and told him to return to the helicopter.

Lee cleared his throat. "Do I need to check the contents of the crates, as well?" The sarcasm in his voice was obvious.

Yu looked at him with a scowl then turned back toward the military helicopter. The soldiers were all assembled inside and the rotors had begun their warm-up rotations. "It is time," Yu said, "to eliminate the trail."

Lee gestured to Wang Sze who stooped and retrieved the extended duffel bag containing the Type 69-I. He quickly unzipped it and took out the grenade launcher, inserted the deadly, cone-shaped projectile and then placed the tube portion over his shoulder so that the exhaust breech extended away from his back. Wang Sze grinned as he looked through the Up-7V telescopic sight. Both Lee and Yu stepped away as the projectile shot forward, leaving an initial trail of grayish smoke that suddenly ignited into a bright propulsion of fire. Lee caught a flash of horror on Cho's face through the windshield in the split second before the rocket completed its trajectory. The helicopter made a quick, forlorn attempt to rise, but was suddenly engulfed in a huge fireball that lit up the deserted airfield.

General Yu watched as the fireball was consumed by the more spectacular secondary explosion as the gas tank ignited. He still held the pistol down by his side and jerked as Lee pressed the cold, hard barrel of a gun against the back of his neck. Lee reached down and snatched the QSZ-92 from Yu's hand.

"You are right," he whispered, placing his face close to the general's right ear. "I knew in the end you would want more than just a bowl of rice."

He took two big steps backward and watched as Wang Sze leaped into the air, his heavily muscled body twisting in midair, his right leg whipping outward with a crescent whirl so fast it seemed blurry in the flickering light of the residual fire.

Lee heard an audible crack as his uncle's head jerked to the left, then almost lazily flopped back to the right. Yu's legs crumpled beneath him as he fell. Wang Sze bounced on his toes, looking down at the fallen general.

"Put him with his faithful servant Cho and the rest of his men," Lee said, and watched as Wang Sze effortlessly picked up Yu's limp body and trotted over to the burning wreckage. Wang Sze's powerful form was silhouetted by the flames as he lifted the general above his head and threw him into the burning wreckage.

The wages of treachery are death, Lee thought as he watched his uncle's body being consumed by the fire. Lee looked at the wicked grin on Wang Sze's face as he ran back and stopped in front of the suitcase and duffel bags.

Lee nodded and smiled as he pointed to the suitcase with the Hong Kong dollars in it. "That one is yours," he said, and pointed to the other bag. "And this one, as well, after you take care of the Americans."

The flickering light from the flames licked over the broad planes of Wang Sze's face as he smiled.

It was, Lee thought, a smile of avarice, but he had no doubt his number-one man would complete the remainder of the task. And as the Americans were being killed, Lee knew he would be far away from Hong Kong, headed toward a new beginning.

At the military section of the airport, Shahkhia watched the workers load the last of the wooden crates into the cargo hold of his chartered Learjet. Lee stood beside him, one of his gangsters at his side, looking a bit nervous. The absence of the bullish bodyguard had piqued the Libyan's interest and he asked about him.

Lee had only shaken his head, saying that Wang Sze was making some final preparations and would be joining them shortly.

Shahkhia wondered what that meant. He had never totally trusted Lee, but had been forced to deal with the devil to obtain the necessary means to achieve his goal…his jihad, as he had now decided to call it. The thoughts of liberating his country and executing those who had sought to bring in the weakening Western influences brought a smile to his lips.

"I take it you are happy now?" Lee asked.

Shahkhia's ruminations returned to the present situation. He still had to complete this part of it. "Yes, very much so. You have arranged for my immediate departure, have you not?"

Lee's expression was coy, but crafty. "I have. I need only give the final instructions and you will be on your way back to Libya." He paused to flash a knowing grin. "With the remainder of your medical and humanitarian supplies."

The Libyan smiled, as well.

"But first," Lee said, "there is a little matter of the final payment."

"But of course." Shahkhia held up his laptop. "However, my computer is in need of some electricity before we can proceed."

Lee said something to his bodyguard in Chinese, and the man trotted down the long hallway toward a series of rooms. He inserted a key into one of the doors and opened it. After glancing inside, he closed the door and ran back to them.

"I have arranged some privacy for us," Lee said. He held out his palm.

Shahkhia nodded and gestured for Sultan to follow. Lee had three more of his men standing by near the hanger. They followed him down the hallway and entered the room. It was rather sparsely furnished, with a desk and some chairs in one corner. A second door stood open and Shahkhia saw a toilet and sink inside. He exchanged a quick, surreptitious glance with Sultan. They had planned this part most carefully and now it was time.

The Libyan went to the desk and, after plugging in his laptop, pressed the on button and waited for the computer to boot up. The desktop came on—the green flag of his homeland—and Mustapha plugged in his modem. Suddenly his head swiveled and he looked at his bodyguard. Lee stood by his side, as nervous as a sacrificial lamb before the preparation of a ceremonial dinner.

Shahkhia hovered over the keyboard, then said to Sultan, "What time is it?"

"Eight-fifteen."

"Where are our rugs?" Shahkhia said. "It is time for prayers."

Sultan nodded and went toward the door.

Lee's head bobbled from one to the other. "Where is your man going now? I thought we were completing our final transaction?"

"We shall," the Arab said, smiling and placing his hand on Lee's shoulder. "But we must be true to our faith. It is time for evening prayer." He watched the Asian devil's lips tighten, but then the man nodded. Shahkhia tried a reassuring smile. "Do not worry, my friend. I will make the transfer now."

He made numerous keystrokes and waited for the appropriate screen to appear. Once that was done, he looked toward Lee and asked, "What is your account number again?"

Lee began to recite it, then stopped and took a pen and paper from a nearby table and wrote the number in block letters. The Libyan took the paper and typed it into his laptop. After a few more keystrokes he pressed the enter button with a flourish and said, "There, it is done." He smiled. "I assume you will want to verify the transaction?"

Lee nodded and began typing on his own computer.

"Ah," Shahkhia said, "before we forget, the clearance?"

Lee flipped open his cell phone. After punching in the number, he began speaking in Chinese.

The Libyan snapped his fingers and shook his head. "Please, in English."

Lee switched languages. "My cargo plane is leaving on runway eight in ten minutes. It has already been inspected, fueled and cleared for takeoff. There are two more passengers to board."

Shahkhia nodded approvingly as the door to the room opened and Sultan came through carrying a large canvas bag. He moved past Lee's bodyguard, then suddenly dropped the bag. As it hit the floor with a thud, Sultan seized the thin Chinese gangster by the head and neck, his enormous hands twisting in different directions simultaneously. An audible snapping sound could be heard and the wispy man fell to the floor, his eyes open but lifeless.

Lee's eyes widened, but before he could react, Shahkhia seized his arms. Sultan closed the distance with a few steps and struck Lee's left temple with a looping hammer punch.

The slender Asian slumped forward, unconscious. Shahkhia's grip held him upright. Sultan grabbed Lee and carried him to the large canvas bag. He opened it, took out a roll of duct tape and began securing Lee's hands behind his back. He placed another square of the tape over Lee's mouth then used more to secure the Asian's arms and legs.

When he had him completely trussed up, he unzipped the bag all the way and removed the rolled rugs. He picked Lee up as easily as he would have lifted a child and set him inside the canvas bag, adjusted the still-unconscious form and then secured the zipper.

"Put the other body in there." Shahkhia pointed to the washroom. He unplugged his computer, closed it and put Lee's computer on top.

Sultan grabbed the dead gangster by the back of the pants and carried him with one hand to the washroom. When he closed the door behind him he held out a pistol he had obviously taken from the dead Chinese.

Shahkhia nodded and smiled. Another gun would always come in handy, as would Mr. Lee as they made their final exit out of Hong Kong.

"IS THAT OUR buddy Eddie Lee?" Grimaldi asked as he and Bolan crouched next to some metal cargo containers on the dock. They were both dressed in black fatigues with dark camo paint on their faces. Grimaldi had taken great care to make his look like tiger stripes.

Bolan continued to study the men getting off the yacht, the *Painted Lady,* as they descended the gangplank. The proportions of the first one were unmistakably familiar—it was Wang Sze. The second man was thinner but wearing a full-brimmed hat—unmistakably Asian, but other than that… It might be Lee, it might not be. Even with the enhanced night-vision binoculars, Bolan couldn't be sure, nor could he be sure that the man who followed was Mustapha Shahkhia. He wore the same wide-brimmed hat, wig and sunglasses Bolan had seen in the surveillance photos.

"Well, is it?" Grimaldi asked again.

"I'm not sure," Bolan replied. "But I'm tired of playing this game."

"Me, too," Grimaldi said. "It's like waiting for the other guy to throw the first punch."

The group of men went into a large warehouse about thirty yards from the dock. Bolan let the night-vision binoculars dangle from the strap around his neck and keyed his throat mike. "Danser, you in position?"

"Affirmative," she said.

"We're going in now," Bolan said, securing the small portable radio to his belt. He removed his Beretta 93-R from the shoulder holster and stood.

Grimaldi stood and unholstered his SIG-Sauer. "Let's do it."

They moved along the dock, staying in the shadows. Bolan came to a narrow passageway between the stacked metal cargo containers. It would take them closer to the warehouse, but it would also be a kill zone if they got caught in the middle. He turned to see Grimaldi assessing the alley, as well.

"What do you think?" Grimaldi asked. "It's a risk."

Bolan nodded, then ran his hand over the side of the corrugated container. He tracked a series of raised metal cleats traveling vertically and pointed. "Let's go this way."

"Up and over," Grimaldi said with a grin. "Love it."

They holstered their weapons and began to climb. When he reached the top Bolan took a quick recce over the edge. He caught a flicker of movement two containers over and ducked. Raising the night-vision binoculars just over the edge, Bolan peered through the lenses and clearly saw two men hunching on the top with submachine guns.

"Looks like they were expecting us," he whispered to Grimaldi, who immediately keyed his throat mike. Bolan did another quick survey of the tops of the adjacent containers. Two more men sat hunched on the far side of the yard perhaps 150 feet away. Bolan waited a few seconds as Grimaldi briefed Danser and the other MI-6 agents about the intended ambush. When Grimaldi finished, he gave a thumbs-up sign and Bolan unleathered the Beretta once more.

A singular, flip-down ocular night-vision piece would make things easier, he thought as he flipped the selector switch to 3-round-burst mode. But as someone once said, you go to war with what you have.

"Ready?" he whispered to Grimaldi.

"I was born ready."

The fingers of Bolan's left hand curled around the top cleat as he braced himself then brought the Beretta up and rested his right arm on the top of the container. He took out the farthest group first with quick bursts, the sound suppressor making little coughing sounds in the darkness. The two closer men whirled and brought their weapons up but the Executioner had already readjusted his aim and zipped a burst through each of them. He scanned the area again through the night-vision binoculars.

It looked clear.

Bolan scaled the rest of the cleats and ran along the top. A space of about six feet separated this first container from the adjacent one and Bolan jumped it with no problem, landing with a catlike grace. Grimaldi landed next to him seconds later with a grunt.

"They should put this in the next Olympics," he said.

Bolan kept moving forward watching the front doors of the warehouse. They suddenly exploded as Danser and her team sent an HE round from a PF-89 grenade launcher smashing into the building. The group of British agents ran forward, each carrying Heckler & Koch MP-5 machine guns that barked rounds, ejected casings and shot fire as a 37 mm gas-round plowed through the shattered opening. As the smoke began billowing out of the doors, Bolan saw a group of retching Chinese exiting, their hands held high above their heads.

"Love that smell of CS gas in the evening," Grimaldi said. "Smells like...victory."

Bolan was still scanning the building and saw a side exit door open. Three coughing men ran through and began making their way through the maze of containers. One of them appeared to be Eddie Lee, the other was wearing the wide-brimmed hat and wig, and the third was unmistakably Wang Sze. Bolan ran forward and jumped to the next container, following their escape route from above. He heard Grimaldi behind him saying, "Why can't this be easy for a change?"

Bolan stopped and glanced down through the narrow passageways formed by the stacked containers. One of the men, the one wearing the wide-brimmed hat, stopped, turned and raised his arm, pointing a gun in Bolan's direction. The Executioner fired a quick burst downward that zipped through the man's torso. He fell to the ground as the other two kept scurrying away. The second man, the one who looked like Eddie Lee, turned and raised his arm. Bolan shot him, as well. Wang Sze was almost at the end of the narrow corridor and had to turn sideways to fit through. As he did so, he turned and fired his pistol in Bolan and Grimaldi's direction. The two men immediately dropped against the container's hard surface.

The muzzle-flashes from Wang Sze's gun lit up the corridor several more times, then abruptly stopped. Bolan extended his arm and fired the Beretta at the big Asian who suddenly disappeared as his gun dropped to the ground.

"You get him?" Grimaldi asked.

Bolan shook his head. "Not sure. You check on those two. I'm going after big boy." He rose to his feet and began to run along the tops of the containers, jumping to the next one when he came to a vacant space. As he got to the edge of the last container, Bolan scanned the area below for movement. About fifty feet away the door to another old warehouse closed with a creaking thud. The soldier immediately descended, using the ladderlike cleats on the side of the container. Running from cover point to cover point, he traversed the distance to the door of the warehouse and paused at the side. He reached to power up his radio to give Grimaldi a heads-up on his position, but realized it was no longer on his belt.

He ripped open the door and swung inside. Moonlight filtered through an immense skylight, illuminating the center of the large building with an eerie glow. High stacks of boxes lined each side, giving the area the look of an arena. Bolan began to move forward, trying to scan the darkened areas between the stacks. He still had the night-vision binoculars and released his left hand from the Beretta to bring up the binoculars just as he heard a creaking sound next to him.

The entire stack of large wooden boxes came careening downward like an oncoming tidal wave. Bolan scrambled forward to get out of the way but was caught in the middle of the chaos. The boxes were made of flimsy wood and were light in weight, but still swept over him, knocking him to the floor, the Beretta slipping from his grasp as he fell.

Bolan rose, throwing off the detritus and flipping open his Espada as he began searching for his gun. He heard a rhythmic thrashing sound and realized seconds later that Wang Sze was running at him from behind. Bolan's peripheral vision caught a glimpse of a flying kick as it collided with his right hip. He tried to roll forward to minimize the impact but was still sent crashing forward into the pile of broken boxes. The knife slipped from his grasp as he tumbled. Bolan continued his roll and got to his feet near a clear area.

The moonlight filtered over the brutish features of the big Chinese as Wang Sze smiled and stepped forward into the light. His shirt was torn, exposing well-developed pectoral muscles and a thick, bullish neck. He continued walking, sidestepping to his left, his jungle-style combat boots making crunching sounds as they glided over the rough concrete floor. He motioned Bolan forward with a palm-down, wiggling-fingers gesture of his right hand.

So, Bolan thought, the big guy wants to fight.

He brought up his hands into a boxing guard and began circling to his right as Wang Sze assumed an orthodox stance. The big Asian moved forward, throwing out his left hand in a feint then whipping a roundhouse kick to Bolan's left thigh. The Executioner stumbled slightly, and Wang Sze threw a quick back fist that smashed against Bolan's left temple. Black dots swarmed in front of his eyes and his knees buckled slightly, but his body reacted automatically and he managed to bounce away on his toes.

Wang Sze stepped forward, but this time Bolan was ready and fired a double left jab into the big Asian's face. The blows stunned him, and the soldier followed up with a right cross that stopped the other man's advance. Smirking, Wang Sze thumbed his nose in a gesture Bolan knew meant derision and stepped forward again. The big American fired off another jab, but the gangster blocked it almost effortlessly and smacked his open palm into the Executioner's face. He pivoted and threw another roundhouse kick, this time with his lead leg, which caught Bolan in the midsection.

Bolan backpedaled, letting his head clear, a stream of red drops from his nose dotting the floor. When Wang Sze rushed forward, the Executioner threw a snapping front kick into the big Asian's chest. The impact of the blow caused him to veer sideways, and Bolan stepped in to deliver a quick one-two punch combination. He followed up with a left hook that smashed into Wang Sze's mouth.

His opponent stumbled backward on unsteady legs for a brief second, blood bubbling from his torn lips, but regained his footing and grinned, his feral teeth a crimson smear.

The two men circled each other cautiously in the glow of the moonlight. Wang Sze feinted again with a flicking back fist, then followed with a spinning kick, but Bolan leaned back and let the other man's foot sail over his shoulder and head. When Wang Sze's foot touched the ground, Bolan stepped inside and delivered a three-punch combination to the gut and sent a right cross to the big Asian's jaw as he backed away.

Wang Sze bent at the waist, his fists brushing the floor, then his head jerked and he straightened.

Bolan saw a flash of wariness in the other man's eyes now and they circled each other again. Wang Sze suddenly leaped forward, his right leg shooting out in a flying kick that caught Bolan in the chest. The stunning force of the blow sent him backward so he rolled with the movement, doing a backward somersault and ending up on his feet. He checked for Wang Sze and saw his opponent had grabbed a long wooden staff from somewhere among the fallen boxes.

Wang Sze smiled again and whirled the staff in a fast figure-eight motion, ending with one end tucked beneath his right armpit, his left hand extended forward. He smiled and motioned Bolan forward again.

Knowing his opponent was obviously well versed in the use of the staff, or bo as it was called in the martial arts, Bolan moved backward, staying out of range while searching for something he could use as a counterweapon. In desperation he grabbed the lid from one of the wood crates and held it up like a shield.

Wang Sze uttered a derisive laugh and moved forward with bold steps, the staff whirling in front of him, smashing into the wooden lid and knocking it from Bolan's grasp. The Executioner tried to get away but the staff collided with his left leg, then his abdomen, then raked down across his back.

Bolan thrust himself forward again, trying to move in the direction of the blow to minimize its force. He was on the floor and managed to roll to his right just in time to avoid a crushing thrust as the end of the staff crunched against the floor next to his head. Bolan swung his feet around, catching Wang Sze's leading leg around the outer edge of the foot and the inside of the thigh. The Executioner used a scissor-like move to send the big Asian sprawling, the staff slipping from his hands. Bolan scrambled over and grabbed the staff just as Wang Sze flipped to his feet with an uncanny grace. He reached forward and grabbed the staff, also, his hands opposite Bolan's. Each man pulled, but Bolan, sensing his foe was probably stronger, moved forward and kicked the other man's left knee. Wang Sze's face contorted and he hunched forward, at which time Bolan smashed his foot into the big Asian's gut, then fell onto his back and executed a perfect judo throw.

Wang Sze went sailing over him and landed with a thump on the floor. Bolan sprang to his feet, gripped the staff in both hands like an oversize baseball bat, and swung for the fence. The end of the staff caught Wang Sze in the left temple and he staggered forward, falling into the shattered boxes on the floor.

Bolan rushed forward to execute a follow-up blow, but saw that none was needed. Wang Sze rolled over on his back, his hands curling around a massive wooden shaft from one of the crates that had impaled him, jutting through his stomach like a bayonet. Blood poured from the edges of the wound as he tried to pull it out. His mouth twisted into a grimace and his breathing hacked with repetitive gasps. He finally managed to pull out the chunk of wood, bringing with it a trail of bloody intestines that continued to flow through the open gash.

Bolan looked down at the man and told him not to move, but saw it was too late. A widening pool of blood began to expand from under Wang Sze, and the big Asian's body stiffened as he went into shock.

Bolan stepped back and began searching for his Beretta 93-R and the Espada. By the time he found them a few minutes later, the eyes of his foe stared back at him with the familiar glaze of death. Bolan walked on unsteady feet toward the door, which burst open as Grimaldi and Danser came hurtling through.

Grimaldi did a quick survey of the scene, zeroing in on the dead Wang Sze and then settling back on Bolan. "You all right, partner?"

"I've been better," Bolan said.

Grimaldi looked at the dead Asian again and shook his head in an appreciative gesture. "Man, looks like I missed one hell of a fight."

"Count your blessings," Bolan said. "I feel like I've been through another war."

Eddie Lee gradually regained consciousness and opened his eyes. He was lying on his left side on a hard surface and his arm was asleep. He flexed his hands and sat up, surprised that he was free from bonds. But something felt strange… unusual. Where was he? Then he knew: on an airplane. He blinked a few times as he surveyed the cabin and saw Mustapha Shahkhia sitting on a long sofalike bench eating a plate of green grapes. The Arab smiled down at him.

"Ah, my friend," he said, "you are awake. Would you care for some refreshments? It is an Arab custom."

Lee felt a pounding in his head as he shook it. The pain was like a searing white light behind his eyes. "Is this how you repay my friendship?"

The Libyan plucked a few more grapes from the vine and tossed them leisurely into his mouth. "We both know the way of the world, my friend. And the money that it takes to keep it revolving." He pointed to Lee's laptop. "We should be in Libya in several hours. Once we have landed, and my plans have proceeded, you will be allowed to earn your release."

Lee stared at him. "At what price?"

Shahkhia smiled again. "As soon as you have returned the money that I transferred to you from my Swiss accounts, of course. Nothing more than what is owed to me."

"We had an agreement," Lee said. The slightest movement

brought more pain inside his head. He brought his hands to his temples. "Have you no honor?"

"Honor. A deal with Satan is one that may be rebuked. Consider it your contribution to the liberation of my country."

Lee didn't try to answer or to move. In his mind he could see the pieces on the *weiqi* board, Shahkhia's black totally surrounding his white. He had grossly underestimated the Arab. The game was all but over, and soon he would be, as well. As he had told himself earlier when dealing with his dear uncle: the wages of treachery were death.

BOLAN STOOD ON the tarmac and watched as Grimaldi went through the final checklist before they took off in the rented Learjet. He knew better than to ask Grimaldi to rush, but they both knew Mustapha Shahkhia had a two-and-a-half-hour head start on them. The thoughts of his last conversation with Hal Brognola flashed through his mind like the endless loop of a repeating audio tape.

"We've got intel that Shahkhia's got a counterinsurgency force already set up on the ground in Libya," Brognola said.

"Can't NATO do an airstrike?" Bolan asked.

"Not until we get something solid that says he's actually got that nerve gas. Right now all we have is a bunch of nomadic tribesmen gathering someplace in the desert. We don't even know where exactly."

"Hopefully," Bolan said, "we'll be able to find that out and call in the cavalry."

"The main thing is to stop him from delivering that damn gas," Brognola said. "I don't have to tell you how much is riding on this, Striker, especially with the UN delegation being in-country."

Brognola told him he'd call back with any further updates, but that had been more than forty minutes earlier. And the clock was ticking double-time.

Danser joined him, looking rather lithe in her black jumpsuit and combat boots.

"Still no word on the whereabouts of Eddie Lee," she said. "One of his men was found dead in the washroom in the military cargo section of the airport. I wish I were going with you."

"We're leaving you with enough of a mess to clean up," he said.

"One partially of our own making." She shook her head. "I can't believe all that's happened in the past two days."

"Sometimes forty-eight hours can be a lifetime," the soldier said. "But you came through like a pro. You can back me up anytime."

She smiled. "You Yanks are pretty damn amazing yourselves, Mr. Cooper, or whatever your name is."

He was about to respond when he heard a whistle and saw Grimaldi waving for him to get aboard. It was departure time.

Bolan extended his hand and after a startled moment she shook it.

"Take care of yourself, Jillian," Bolan said. "Maybe our paths will cross again sometime."

"I certainly hope so," she said. Her eyes misted over. "Good luck and godspeed."

We'll need it, Bolan thought as he trotted up the steps and into the jet, shaking off the residual soreness of his fight with Wang Sze.

He pressed the button to retract the steps and then pulled the pressurized door closed and secured it. He joined Grimaldi in the cockpit. They saw Danser waving vigorously to them as Grimaldi began to warm up the engines.

"She looks pretty hot in that black jumpsuit, doesn't she?" he said, his hand lingering on the throttle. "Kind of makes me regret we didn't have another night to spend in good old Hong Kong."

"Yeah," Bolan said, giving her a final wave as she swung

out of view. "But look on the bright side. We're going to Libya and now you might get a chance to see Celise Boyer."

Grimaldi's face took on a contemplative expression. "You think so?"

"Plus," Bolan said, "Hal arranged to have *Dragonslayer* shipped to Libya. With any luck she'll be there in time for you to use on the mission."

Grimaldi grinned and gunned the engines, moving the plane down the tarmac to takeoff position. "Hot damn, what are we waiting for?"

A THIN LAYER of dust blew across the landing strip as Mustapha Shahkhia descended the metal stairs of the jet and stepped back on Libyan soil for the first time in months. He immediately dropped to his knees, gave thanks to God and kissed the earth. When he rose he saw his trusted uncle Omar standing in front of him, his long, flowing robe blocking out the distant vestiges of the setting sun.

"Glory be to God," Shahkhia said as he embraced Omar and kissed his cheeks.

Omar repeated the greeting. When the two men separated, the older one asked, "You have the rest of the gas?"

Shahkhia nodded and barked an order for the men to begin unloading the cargo, then to secure a camouflage tarp over the plane. They were in the vast desert area between Surt and Bani Walid—the area informally known as *jahannam*—Arabic for "hell" but near the birthplace of the Great Leader, his true father. It was also the place where the Americans had killed Colonel Ahad Shahkhia, his other father. He felt a kinship to these desert sands and felt it was somehow appropriate that he launch his jihad against the Great Satan from this place. It was God's will.

"Forgive me, nephew," Omar said. "I should have invited you to my tent to refresh yourself after your long journey."

Shahkhia shook his head dismissively. "What progress have you made since we last talked?"

Omar smiled. "We have almost completed the assembly of the drones. Once we have the two parts of the Sleeping Dragons united, we will be ready."

"And you have the vehicles, as I instructed?"

"Of course, nephew," Omar said. He turned and pointed to a line of pickups, vans and a military Humvee with a long antenna extending from its right rear fender. "It is equipped with a field radio so we will know exactly when to commence the launch."

Shahkhia nodded and watched as Eddie Lee was escorted down the steps of the jet. Sultan followed, and his master snapped his fingers and motioned to him. The giant descend the steps and strode over.

"Yes, sir."

"Have the Chinese taken to my tent. Have him make sure those technicians he gave us have the computers set to pilot the drones. Then you must proceed immediately to Tripoli and collect the hostages." Sultan gave a slight bow of respect.

Shahkhia nodded in reply but kept his eyes locked on the other man. "Do not return without the UN hostages and that evil woman."

Sultan bowed again and said, "On my honor, your will shall be done."

BOTH BOLAN AND GRIMALDI felt like they were running on caffeine and adrenaline by the time they landed in Greece and hopped the interim plane that took them to the USS *Guadalcanal,* the U.S. Navy aircraft carrier where Brognola had delivered *Dragonslayer.* Grimaldi's face lost all traces of fatigue as he looked at the big helicopter's sleek lines and polished steel surface. He immediately went to inspect "his baby" while Bolan called Stony Man Farm on his sat phone. Brognola's voice sounded gruff and grim, as usual.

"You sound beat," Bolan said. "You getting any sleep?"

"Probably about as much as you," Brognola replied. "Where are you?"

"We're on the carrier. Jack's checking out *Dragonslayer.* I called for a sitrep."

Bolan heard Brognola's heavy sigh. "Things aren't looking too good. We still haven't been able to pinpoint Mustapha Shahkhia's whereabouts, although we're sure he's now in Libya. Remember Maria Noval from your little stint in Mexico a couple of days ago?"

"Yeah. What about her?"

"Well, her father works for the company that has the contract to build our Predator drones. He's provided us with some frequencies we're monitoring right now to try to pinpoint Shahkhia's location. He's got to have some kind of broadcast center set up. If we can find out where he's hiding, the President's authorized an airstrike from the carrier."

Bolan considered that. "It'd be a lot easier than Jack and me flying around the desert looking for a needle in a haystack."

"I'd settle for just finding the haystack. Anyway, we've got another little fly in the ointment." Brognola paused. "I assume you know about that movie star who's visiting with the UN delegation as some sort of human-rights ambassador?"

"Yeah, Celise Boyer," Bolan said. "Jack's got the hots for her."

"Well, he's going to get the chance to meet her, up close and personal. Our latest intel suggests that someone's been watching her hotel for the past two days."

"You're thinking that Shahkhia's going to grab a little insurance against any NATO retaliation once he launches the attack?"

"That's the most logical assumption," Brognola said. "So we need someone to go in and get her and the rest of the delegation and take them back to the carrier."

"Sounds like a job for SEAL Team Six."

"They've already been deployed in the desert looking for the chemical weapons. Can you handle it? In the meantime, we'll keep trying to pinpoint Shahkhia."

"Sounds like a plan," Bolan said.

Bolan joined the Stony Man pilot a few minutes later.

"What are you smiling at?" Grimaldi asked as he continued going through his preflight checklist.

"You seem to be in a good mood and I was just wondering if your grin could get any broader," Bolan said.

"Only if I could get a date with Celise Boyer while we're here."

"Well, just remember," Bolan said, "you should always be careful what you wish for."

Abdul Sultan sat in the Humvee in the darkened alley in the center of Tripoli, several blocks away from the Crown International Hotel, and waited. At least the vehicle was large enough to accommodate his oversize frame. Not many were, and he made a mental note to ask his boss if he could keep it for his own use during the coming days.

He debated whether to use the field radio in the vehicle to brief Shahkhia of his arrival, or wait until he had the American woman and the other infidels in custody, as his sheikh had instructed. Using the radio raised the possibility of the Americans tracing the signal back to their base. Sultan did not know if the American dogs were that close, but it was best to assume they were.

The capital looked tranquil through the windshield, showing only darkened buildings and a few glowing lights, but soon he knew it would be transformed into a roiling sea of death. Death to the traitors. He had only to complete this final task and the liberation would begin.

The sound of the motorcycle's engine wound through the alley. He saw the single headlight as it turned in from the street. Sultan rolled down the left rear window and waited as the motorcycle rider came to a stop next to the Humvee.

"Glory be to God," the rider said. He wore a robe and had a dark scarf wrapped around his face.

Sultan returned the greeting and asked for an update.

"They are all in the hotel," the rider said. "They have taken the entire fifth floor."

Sultan nodded. "You have done well."

"There is more. The American woman takes one of the security men down to the rear alley each night at 8:15. She purchases illegal liquor from one of the black marketeers."

Illegal liquor, Sultan thought. How appropriate these infidels will be undone by their filthy dissipations. He glanced at his watch. It was seven minutes to eight. Perfect.

"Get ready," he said to his driver. "We move now."

"WHICH HOTEL IS she at?" Grimaldi asked as he piloted *Dragonslayer* over the dark water toward the lighted port city. He and Bolan had already hooked up their radios and earpieces so they could communicate despite the noise from the powerful rotors.

"The Crown International," Bolan said. "Think you can land this thing on the roof?"

Grimadli smirked. "I could land this baby on a golf tee sitting on a barge floating in the middle of Lake Michigan during a thunderstorm."

Bolan grinned. "Just the same, I'll rappel first and clear the LZ."

Grimaldi nodded. "I wouldn't have it any other way. Now sit back and relax. We'll be there in ten."

Bolan glanced at his watch—8:00 p.m. Hopefully, this would go by the numbers: rappel to the roof, clear the landing zone, land the chopper, establish contact with the security detail and bring the delegates and Ms. Celise Boyer up to the roof for a quick, surreptitious dust-off. Then they could get back to tracking down Mustapha Shahkhia and the Sleeping Dragons.

That was the imperative: to end this thing quickly before the gas could be used. Visions of the previous times he'd seen the brutal effects of nerve gas clicked through his memory like an ongoing horror show depicting the herky-jerk motions of the bloody, frothy death throes. But he was confident Shahkhia wouldn't launch the drones until he was sure he had the hostages as his insurance against a U.S. retaliation.

"How many we picking up again?" Grimaldi asked.

"Thirteen. Five UN delegates, your girlfriend Celise, her hairdresser, two TV news guys and the four security men." Bolan pondered what else Brognola had told him during the phone briefing. "And guess who the security men are."

Grimaldi flashed him a questioning glance.

"The same group of Bearcats we had on the Monterrey mission," Bolan said. "Minus Dominguez, of course. He's the one who was wounded."

"Well, what do you know? It's a small world, after all," Grimaldi said. "In fact..." He reached over and pressed a button on the console and the song of the same name began to play in their earpieces.

"I've always hated that damn song," Bolan said, looking at him as he slipped on a small backpack.

"I know," Grimaldi said, grinning. "Why do you think I downloaded it?"

SULTAN HEARD THE SOUND of the helicopter slicing through the night sky as they approached the mouth of the alley where the American woman was supposed to be. It had to be the Americans coming. Did they receive word of the abduction plan? His ears strained, but he was certain he only heard one helicopter. Surely the Americans, if they planned to intercede, would send dozens. His watch read 8:10.

"The rest of you go up now and get the ones on the fifth floor," he said. "We will wait here and get the woman."

Ten of his men, all clad in dark clothing and face scarves, their AK-47s concealed under heavy robes, began filing along the side of the building toward the main entrance to the hotel.

BOLAN HAD JUST finished securing the knotted nylon rope to the cleat on the side of the helicopter's open door when he heard the first shots, followed by more sporadic gunfire.

M-4s versus Kalashnikovs, he thought, judging from the sound. The good guys versus the bad guys. That means the party had already started.

"On rappel," he said into his throat mike.

"Roger that," Grimaldi said. "Steady as she goes."

Bolan lined up on the edge of the door, his back facing the dark sky, as he looped the rope through his D-ring and shook it loose out the door. It unraveled downward into the darkness like a gyrating snake. He stepped out onto the solid rung, lowered himself backward until he was almost suspended upside down, his head well below the edge of the landing strut to avoid getting struck, and shoved off.

His body zipped downward, spinning a few times as the twisted rope straightened, until he stopped his descent a few feet from the rooftop. Bolan unhooked from the line and shone his flashlight around. The hotel helipad was to the far right, just as Aaron Kurtzman's intel said it would be. He moved over to use his powerful flashlight as a guide beacon and directed Grimaldi's landing descent.

As the big helicopter touched down, Bolan keyed his throat mike again.

"It sounds like the party's started without us down there," he said. "I'll be back in a flash."

"Roger that," Grimaldi said. "And I'll be waiting."

Bolan ran to the roof exit and tried the knob. Locked. Not wanting to waste any more time, he slipped off the backpack and took out a medium-size crowbar he'd stowed for just such an occasion. Jamming the bladed edge between the door and the jamb, just above the knob, he pressed hard with all his strength, all the while listening to the escalating gunfire. Once the crowbar was securely inserted, he shoved with all his strength. The lock popped as the door jerked open. He dropped the crowbar on the pebbled roof and looked into the narrow expanse in front of him. More gunshots echoed.

The staircase was narrow but lighted. Bolan unleathered his Beretta 93-R as he raced down the stairs. He knew the UN delegation had reserved the entire fifth floor and the hotel had twelve floors.

When he got to the sixth floor he glanced over the railing and saw two men with AK-47s standing on the landing. Bolan moved down to the intermediate space between the floors where he had a clear shot and took both of them out with two quick silenced bursts. He then ran down the remaining stairs and rolled the bodies away from the door so he could take a quick look. A group of men in dark robes and wielding AK-47s stood bunched together in the hallway, the air full of cordite fumes and smoke.

Bolan opened the door a crack so he could execute a fast, deadly burst. As his rounds zipped through the backs of the assailants, a few in the front of the group realized the new threat and started to turn, but it made no difference. In less than seven seconds they all lay strewed on the floor.

The Executioner ducked back into the stairwell and did a combat reload. He moved his head to the doorway for another quick look.

No active threats, but he did see what appeared to be an American face looking out from a doorway about fifty feet down the corridor, the black barrel of an M-4 rifle protruding slightly in front.

"Hey, Bearcat," Bolan called out. "How many more hostiles we got?"

The face did a double take, then came a voice tinged with familiarity. "Sir, is that you?"

It was Tom Lipinski. Bolan remembered the kid's familiar whine from the training sessions where he complained about having to cut the cyclone fence each time.

"What did I tell you about calling me 'sir'?" Bolan said,

then took a chance and exposed more of himself around the doorjamb. "How many hostiles left?"

Lipinski blinked and shook his head. "We already took out two, si—Sarge. There might be more downstairs."

Bolan did another check of both directions of the hallway and asked Lipinski if he had all the civilians ready.

"All but Ms. Boyer and Kevin," Lipinski said. "They went downstairs to the back door to meet somebody."

Kevin? Kevin Norris, the hot dog of the group. Bolan swore but didn't waste time with any more questions about the situation. It was what it was. He gave Lipinski quick instructions to get everyone up to the roof for departure then keyed his mike.

"I'm sending three Bearcats up to you with the civilians," he told Grimaldi. "I've got to go downstairs to collect two more people."

"What about Celise?" Grimaldi asked.

"She's one of them," Bolan said, slapping Lipinski's shoulder as the kid ran through the doorway leading a group of terrified-looking diplomats. He tapped German Valdez, the other familiar Bearcat, as he passed, as well. The kid tried to smile, but looked grim. Bolan watched as they all double-timed up the stairs, then he started down the stairwell toward the lobby.

Sultan decided it was prudent to kill the American male, whom he took for a soldier of some sort, although not much of one judging by how easy it had been to surprise him and the woman. Sultan pressed his pistol against the man's forehead and pulled the trigger. The American's head jerked backward and he fell onto the ground as the American woman screamed and the Libyan black-market traitor looked on in surprise and horror.

Sultan reached forward and grabbed the woman by her long hair and pulled her to her knees next to him. Then he aimed the pistol and shot the traitor in the face, as well. The blood spurted out like a fountain from the man's open mouth, covering both Abdul and Celise Boyer. The blood of his enemy was like the blood of a pig, except in battle when it became a badge of honor. The woman screamed again, and he doubled his grip in the long hair to pull her along.

It is fitting to do this, he thought, *to a woman who exposes herself so wantonly.*

"Come," he said to his driver. "Get her to the vehicle. We will meet the others at the rendezvous point."

BOLAN PAUSED TO check the body, which he recognized as Bearcat Kevin Norris, as he moved into the alley behind the hotel. The man's dead eyes stared up at him and Bolan could feel no pulse. The facial wound looked nonsurvivable.

Poor kid, Bolan thought. He learned things the hard way, but deserved better.

He heard a woman's scream and raced to the end of the alley.

A huge man was attempting to stuff a squirming woman into the rear door of a large black Humvee.

From what he could see, the woman was Celise Boyer.

Bolan raised his Beretta to fire when the whining roar of a motorcycle suddenly bore down on him from behind. He whirled in time to see a man wearing a dark scarf over his face, leaving only his eyes visible, about twenty feet away on some kind of a black motorcycle. The soldier acquired his sight picture and fired. The man's head jerked back, and he tumbled to the side as the out-of-control vehicle continued to careen toward Bolan.

He glanced back, trying to draw a bead on the big guy by the Humvee, but it was too late. The left rear door slammed shut and the vehicle took off down the street. Bolan jumped out of the way as the motorcycle crashed into a pile of garbage cans, knocking them down and spewing their contents all over. The driver lay a few feet away in a twisted heap. Bolan picked up the vehicle and climbed onto the seat, keying his mike to call Grimaldi.

"Sitrep," he said.

"We're all on board up here," Grimaldi said. "You find her?"

"Working on it," Bolan replied. "One Bearcat down for the count here. I have to go mobile. Leave without me. I'll call you for a ride once I get her."

"Roger that." Bolan could detect the concern in Grimaldi's tone but didn't waste any more words. He adjusted his grip on the Beretta so that he could twist the accelerator. The motorcycle shot forward, and Bolan managed to catch a glimpse of the Humvee on the street about a hundred yards ahead of him. He kicked the shift lever into Second and popped the clutch. The motorcycle's engine screamed as the soldier wound it up to the limit before depressing the clutch and tapping it into third gear. It shot forward like a rocket, and he could tell he had closed the distance between him and the Humvee by at least half.

He twisted the accelerator to the maximum and came within twenty feet of the vehicle. Bolan shifted again with a calculated quickness, then transferred the Beretta to his left hand and shot out the left rear tire. The Humvee zigzagged but kept going, the tire sounding like a jackhammer gone wild as the ragged flap beat against the pavement with each revolution.

Bolan twisted the accelerator and pulled up alongside the driver's window. Raising the Beretta, he fired two quick bursts through the glass and veered away just as the Humvee's front fender swung toward him.

He lost his grip on the Beretta as he tried to stabilize the motorcycle, which had begun to sway from side to side like a buoy on a choppy sea. In his peripheral vision he caught sight of the Beretta tumbling past his left foot and bouncing several times on hard pavement. He managed to stabilize the bike as it went into a long skid, twisting the front wheel so that the steel-ribbed frame hit the ground first followed by his body.

The inertial force propelled him forward and he felt the grinding friction of the asphalt tearing off the left sleeve and pantleg of his fatigues then grabbing at his flesh. The motorcycle came to rest on the gravel shoulder of the road, but the momentum slung him several more feet and he rolled over and over before coming to a stop. He managed one moderately deep breath before the wave of pain swept over him.

The Humvee, in the meantime, had crashed into a cinderblock wall about twenty yards away and come to rest.

Bolan shook his head gingerly to try to restore his equilibrium. The right rear door of the Humvee flopped open and a giant leg protruded. The big man moved unsteadily as he extricated himself from the vehicle and then turned, reaching inside, and began pulling Celise Boyer from the rear seat compartment.

Bolan rose to his feet as he heard her scream, his eyes futilely scanning the ground for the lost Beretta. His legs and feet felt numb under him, but he forced them to move. One step, two, three...drunkenly at first... He was running now, perhaps three yards from the big man. Bolan hoped he had enough strength left to use his arms.

The giant's face twisted into a snarl, and he released the squirming woman and raised his pistol, aiming in Bolan's direction.

The adrenaline surge took over as the Executioner spotted a shredded hunk of tread from the ruined tire on the street in front of him. He reached down and in one motion hurled the tread in a sidearm pitch. The black tread went end over end until it smashed into the giant's face The big man jerked as if he'd been hit by a baseball bat.

The bright flash from the errant shot from the giant's pistol seared the left side of Bolan's face. The Executioner was there in two more steps and slammed the big man's gun hand into the door post of the Humvee. The pistol tumbled from the huge man's grip. Bolan followed up with a back fist to his opponent's face, then tried to pull him off balance to execute a judo throw. The giant recovered in time and gave Bolan a powerful shove that drove him back several feet.

The giant's mouth twisted into a fierce scowl as he pulled out a long *jambiya* and said, "I will slit your throat, you American dog."

Bolan reached back with his right hand and grasped the handle of his folding knife. As he made his next two steps, regaining his balance, he flipped open the blade. The giant's knife was much larger, leaving a disparity of at least four inches over Bolan's. The big man grinned.

What I lack in size, the soldier thought, I can hopefully make up in speed.

The giant moved forward, making a huge arcing slash with the *jambiya*. Bolan backpedaled, avoiding the swing, and brought up his own knife with a slashing movement, catching the inner aspect of the giant's right wrist.

The giant swung again, and Bolan leaned back, avoiding most of the force of the blow, but the *jambiya* sliced open his left shoulder.

"Is that the best you can do?" Bolan said, trying to put as much derision into his voice as possible.

Enraged, the giant swung the *jambiya* again, this time using a backhanded thrust. Bolan timed the move and stepped inside, slashing with the Espada. The blade tore the sleeve of giant's forearm. Blood seeped through the material.

The giant swore in Arabic, and Bolan returned the insult. As the big man moved forward, slashing downward, Bolan sidestepped then did a short stutter step forward using a downward motion that caught the giant's right upper arm. The Executioner immediately zipped the blade back again, slicing over the big man's forearm. The giant jerked forward, and Bolan slashed upward with his knife, catching his assailant's throat. The giant dropped the *jambiya* and brought both of his hands to his neck, trying to stem the crimson flow that cascaded from the gash across his neck.

"You dog," the giant managed to croak.

Bolan remained silent, stepping in close to deliver the kill stroke.

The giant tried to speak again, but only a bloody gurgle emanated from his parted lips. The man-mountain continued to stagger toward Bolan, like a man on a bender, then pitched forward as his legs tangled and he fell, taking the Executioner to the asphalt. He kicked and twisted his way out from under the giant's carcass. The big man lay facedown on the street, twin pools of dark liquid expanding from either side of his thick neck like a broken water main.

Bolan surveyed the interior of the Humvee. The driver was crumpled on the front seat, his face a mixture of blood and shattered glass. Celise Boyer had crawled back into the vehicle and cowered in the far corner of the backseat next to an old-fashioned field radio that kept blasting transmissions in Arabic. At least he thought it was her. The feminine face was wan and drawn, with black streaks of mascara smeared in vertical lines over the fine cheekbones. Her long brown hair was a tangled mess.

Bolan reached out and patted the woman's leg, saying, "You're all right, ma'am. You're safe now. I'm an American and I'm taking you home."

Her eyes were still wide with terror, but she managed a nod.

Suddenly, Bolan heard the sounds of a car screeching to a stop across the street. Three men in robes and face scarves jumped out of the vehicle and began firing pistols at the Humvee. One round shattered the window next to his head, and Bolan yelled for Celise Boyer to "Get on the floor" as he stooped and picked up the gun the giant had dropped. It was a Chinese Type QSZ-92.

Bolan brought it up, pointed and squeezed the trigger. The first of the three men jerked as the round hit him in the chest. He staggered into the second man just as the soldier's next shot struck that man in the neck. Bolan adjusted his sight picture and squeezed off two more rounds into the third man, one in the chest and one in the head. For good measure he put a round in each of the other two fallen assailants as they lay prone on the asphalt and quickly checked the rest of the area. The doors of the car stood open. It was empty. Nothing moved. He snapped on the safety and stuck the pistol into his belt. This one was a keeper. Bolan turned back to check Celise Boyer.

Her eyes were wide with terror. "You…you killed them."

Bolan ignored her and instead concentrated on the old-style field radio inside the rear of the Humvee. An orange LED lit up with each transmission it received.

"Abdul, Abdul, this is Sheikh Mustapha. Are you there?" the voice blasted in Arabic from the field radio speaker. "Do you have the hostages? Do you have the woman? The drones are ready for launch."

Bolan keyed his throat mike, and Grimaldi answered with, "What's up?"

"You still in radio communication with the carrier?" Bolan asked.

"You bet."

"Are they still trying to pinpoint Mustapha Shahkhia?"

"As far as I know," Grimaldi said. "The beautiful part about it is all we have to do is find him and there's a couple of cruise missiles and a squadron of F-18 Super Hornet already up in the air ready and waiting to do the job."

"Have them home in on this frequency," Bolan said, shining his flashlight over the numbers above the field radio selector dial.

He read off the frequency and said, "Tell them to triangulate for Shahkhia's base position."

"Roger that." Grimaldi's laugh came over the earpiece. "Any other miracles you want to pull off while you're at it?"

"Just one," Bolan said, picking up the microphone for the field radio and depressing the transmit button.

EDDIE LEE WATCHED Mustapha Shahkhia shouting into the old field radio. The man was screaming in Arabic. Lee was able to distinguish the name "Abdul" in the speech, but little else. Obviously, he was trying to establish contact with the giant. Lee's fingers absently made creases in the torn piece of notebook paper he'd found. The Arabic scrawl on it was meaningless to him, but at least it afforded him the opportunity to make one more folded paper dragon. Perhaps it would be his last. He doubted that the Libyan would let him live once he'd transferred the money out of his Cayman accounts. Even if the Arab did release him, Lee knew he was still trapped in the middle of some desert hell.

I will never get back to Hong Kong, he thought as he made the penultimate fold in the paper. And even if I did, I am a marked man there, as well.

"Abdul, Abdul," Shahkhia yelled into the microphone. Lee thought the Arab was a mad dog.

Lee made the final fold in the paper—his last dragon—and heard a mottled reply transmitted on the field radio.

Shahkhia grew excited and answered.

The mottled reply came again, more distinct this time. But it didn't sound like Arabic. It almost sounded like English.

Lee saw the Libyan's brow furrow, his dark eyes staring intently at the old boxlike radio.

"Abdul, is that you?" he asked in English.

"No," came the reply, also in English. "It isn't."

"You American dog," Shahkhia shouted. "Prepare to die."

"You first," the American said.

Seconds later Lee heard the sound of a whistling roar... Something was approaching, like the roll of distant thunder, and then another. Lee knew immediately what they were. He held the dragon tightly in his hand, looked at Mustapha Shahkhia and smiled. The Arab's face twisted into a fear-laden grimace. He, too, knew what was approaching. American cruise missiles.

The Americans had found his base.

Epilogue

Bolan felt like he'd been through the wringer as he lay prone on the crisp white sheets in sick bay clad only in a hospital smock as the pretty female nurse applied generous amounts of antibacterial ointment to the Libyan road rash on his left arm, leg and backside. His right shoulder had a four-inch-long track of stitches where the knife wound had been sewn shut.

Although the metal walls of the examination room were gunmetal-gray, he could hardly tell he was on board a ship. Of course this particular ship was as large as a small city. The doctor stood a few feet away studying a pair of X-rays on a lighted screen. Bolan pressed the sat phone to his ear as Brognola continued with his postmission debriefing.

"So as I was telling you," he said, "the cruise missiles and Super Hornets zeroed in on those coordinates you gave them and were able to take out all of Shahkhia's little drone air force. Then the SEALs moved in and cleaned out the rest."

"They get a confirmation on Shahkhia?" Bolan asked.

"You bet," Brognola said. "They also found the body of an unidentified Asian male believed to be Eddie Lee, which fits. Nobody's seen hide nor hair of him in Hong Kong."

"Strange that he'd come here with the Libyan," Bolan said. "But then again, he might not have had any choice."

"It appears that when the cruise missiles hit, the explosion caused a minidisbursement of the Sleeping Dragons around the camp. You might say that Shahkhia got hoisted with his own petard."

"Shakespeare would have approved," Bolan said.

Bognola was silent for a moment, then said, "I know I don't say this often enough, but you guys did good."

"Well, on that note, I'll bid you adieu," Bolan said. "It looks like the doc's finished checking out my X-rays." After a quick goodbye, he terminated the call.

"Well," the doctor said, "miraculously, I don't see any broken bones."

"He's too damn mean to break anything," Grimaldi said as he strode into the room.

The doctor seemed about to say something when Bolan waved his hand and said, "It's okay, Doc. I know him."

The doctor's eyebrows rose like twin caterpillars and he remained silent for a moment, then continued. "As I said, no broken bones, but you've got enough contusions and abrasions over your entire body that you'll probably look like the illustrated man for a few weeks."

"The illustrated man?" Grimaldi said. "Wasn't that an old movie, or something?"

"Yeah, and a book, too," Bolan said. "By Ray Bradbury."

"Right, I remember." Grimaldi clapped his hands together. "So, partner, you ready to get out of here? *Dragonslayer*'s all gassed up and Aaron's got a C-130 waiting for us in Greece to fly us Stateside."

"Stateside? All I want to do is sleep for a week."

"Once we get on that C-130 you can catch all the z's you want on the way back to Virginia." Grimaldi flashed him a grin. Sensing an ulterior motive somewhere, Bolan grinned back.

"What's the rush? You said you wanted to show Celise Boyer the inside of *Dragonslayer?*"

"I did." Grimaldi's grin twisted into a grimace and he

ducked and looked around. "And don't say that name too loud. She might pop up in here."

"Would that be a bad thing?" Bolan asked. "I thought you had an extreme case of the hots for her?"

The nurse's eyes shot from Bolan to Grimaldi and back to Bolan as she smiled. "Him and all the 4,568 male sailors on this ship."

Grimaldi did another quick look around then leaned close. "Yeah, well, they can have her."

"What do you mean?" Bolan asked.

Grimaldi's frown deepened. "You see what she looks like without her customary ton of makeup? Not to mention that all she did the whole time since we got back from Tripoli was moan and complain about why you couldn't shoot to wound instead of kill, like they do in the movies. And this was after you rescued her sorry ass."

"In a way it's understandable," Bolan said with a grin. "Didn't her actor boyfriend star in a remake of *The Lone Ranger?*"

"Whatever," Grimaldi said. "But anyway, that's not the worst of it. You don't know the whole story."

"Well, fill me in."

Grimaldi sighed. "After you got out of *Dragonslayer* I sort of invited her up to the cockpit with me, you know, just trying to be nice."

"Yeah, I remember." Bolan gave him an exaggerated wink. "And?"

"And she upchucked all over the place."

"She'd been through a lot," Bolan said.

"Yeah, yeah, I know."

"Didn't that happen in the movie?" Bolan asked, trying not to smile. *"Peppermill?"*

"Man, what a mess," Grimaldi said, shaking his head. "And guess who had to clean it all up."

"Builds character," Bolan said, smiling broadly.

"Yeah, well, if there's two things in life you don't do," Grimaldi replied, holding up his index finger, "it's diss my buddy for saving your life and not being the Lone Ranger." He held up a second finger, looked at it and frowned. "And then toss your cookies in *Dragonslayer.*"

Bolan laughed out loud. "Yeah, that's for sure," he said, "you don't mess with another man's baby, especially not *Dragonslayer.*"

The nurse giggled.

"Well, what do you think, partner?" Grimaldi asked. "You ready to roll?"

Bolan tried to think of a clever reply, but was way too tired. Instead, he just nodded and heaved a sigh as he turned his head up toward the nurse and asked, "Nurse, do you think you can find me a clean shirt and another pair of pants?"

"I should be able to do that," she said, "but are you sure you're ready?"

Grimaldi started to say something, but Bolan cut him off.

"Ready?" he said with a quick wink. "My partner here was *born* ready." He turned his head back to Grimaldi. "But why don't you see if Celise Boyer might want to come with us? You could finish showing her *Dragonslayer.*"

A red flush started to creep up Grimaldi's neck to his face.

Bolan enjoyed a moment of watching his friend squirm. Their banter was a welcome break from the Executioner's War Everlasting. Soon enough the battlefield would call them into action again. For now they would share this moment of camaraderie.

* * * * *